THE HAUNTED MUSEUM

THE PEARL EARRING

BOOK THREE

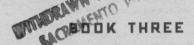
Suzanne Weyn

SCHOLASTIC INC.

For lovers of spooky stories everywhere.

ISBN 978-0-545-58847-8

12 11 10 9 8 7 6 5 4 3 2 1   15 16 17 18 19 20/0

Printed in the U.S.A.   40
First printing, January 2015

The text type was set in Old Style 7.
Book design by Abby Kuperstock

INTRODUCTION

WELCOME. You have arrived at the Haunted Museum.
It's a place where dreams are made — bad dreams!
Ghostly phantasms float. When you least expect it,
a hand grabs your throat. A jar falls and unleashes
an ancient curse.

I opened the Haunted Museum many, *many* years
ago. And I've been adding to its special displays for
longer than I can recall.

Some say the museum has become a worldwide

chain — just an entertaining fraud for the amusement of tourists.

Others see something more mysterious, more sinister within its walls.

Either way, no one escapes unaffected by what they find within the museum. The items that touch your hands will come back to touch your life in a most terrifying manner.

Take, for instance, the case of Lily Powers, who has dreams of becoming a model. When she's asked to pose by an artist whose portraits hang on the Haunted Museum walls, she jumps at the chance. But she soon learns that there's something more to these paintings than meets the eye — something horrifying.

Happy Haunting,

Belladonna Bloodstone

Founder and Head Curator

THE HAUNTED MUSEUM

1

BYE, MOM!" Lily Powers waved from the curb as her mother disappeared into a yellow cab. Mrs. Powers was on her way to the airport. That day she would fly to a college in Ohio where she had been hired to teach a summer class in art history.

Lily had been dreading another boring summer on another boring college campus, so she was thrilled to find herself in New York City instead. She turned to her aunt Amy who stood beside her. "I can't believe Mom will be gone for a whole month."

"It's just you and me now, kiddo," Lily's aunt Amy said with a smile. "Think you can stand being with me for all that time?"

Lily was sure she could. In fact, she was looking forward to it. Amy was more like a cool best friend than a parent. At twenty-three, wearing skinny jeans, a tank top adorned with the logo of her favorite rock band, lots of plastic bracelets, and short, spiky, bright red hair, Amy was Lily's idea of the ultimate young city dweller. "I can't believe your mom trusted me to take care of you," Amy added.

"Me neither," Lily said.

Amy scowled at her. "Hey! I resent that. I'm an adult, you know. Gainfully employed, even."

Lily laughed. "I didn't mean anything bad by it. It's just that Mom is so fussy about things and you're . . . kind of not."

"I know," Amy agreed. "We'll have a good time. We can bike around Central Park, and there's a cool Jasper Johns exhibit at MoMA."

"MoMA?" Lily asked.

"Museum of Modern Art," Amy explained. "It's in midtown, but we can take the subway. While we're up there, we'll snag tickets at the Radio City box office. Mumford and Sons are playing there next month."

"I love them," Lily said excitedly. "My friends and I just found some good concert videos on YouTube I could show you."

"I can't really access the Internet right now," Amy said.

"I can help you with that. I'm pretty good with computer stuff. Does the router need to be reset?"

"There's nothing you could really do to fix this problem."

What could the problem be? "You do *have* Internet, don't you?" Lily asked.

"Sort of. I mean, I *used* to have Internet but I didn't pay last month's bill so the cable company shut it off."

No Internet?! "When will it be turned back on?"

"When I pay the bill."

"Are you paying it soon?" Lily asked.

"It depends what you mean by *soon*," Amy replied in an apologetic tone.

Lily tried to hide her disappointment. But hopefully they wouldn't be spending a month at Amy's apartment without Internet.

"My roommate, Sylvia, is gone for the summer," Amy added. "She got this great job teaching English in India, but I can't ask her to split the bills like we usually do, since she's away. I probably won't be able to pay the bill until she gets back in September."

Lily didn't want to make her aunt feel bad, though. "It'll be all right," she said cheerfully. "If I need to go online I'll go to a diner or a library where they have an Internet connection," Lily suggested.

Amy grimaced and looked even more apologetic. "I feel bad about this but you'll have to stay in the apartment while I'm at work." Amy worked in the art department of a fashion magazine called *Swirl*, designing the look of the photos and the layout of text on the pages. "Maybe you could come into my office and do some filing for a few days."

"Filing?!" Lily said with a groan. That was her big treat?

Amy sighed. "Sorry, kiddo. The only way I can bring you to work is if you file or run errands or something. I can't let you go wandering around the city on your own. It wouldn't be responsible, and I don't want to let your mother down."

"I'm not a baby!" Lily complained. She'd pictured a week of exploring the city: going to shops, museums, shows. Hanging out within a two-block radius of Amy's apartment wasn't even close to the way she'd envisioned her summer. "How am I going to stay inside for three weeks?!" she cried.

"Well, there's plenty to do near my building, and I'll be home by five-fifteen."

"That's eight hours!"

"Let me think about it," Amy said with a sigh. "Maybe we can find something for you to do in the day."

"I hope so," Lily said.

"Anyway, the good thing about Sylvia being gone is that we'll have more room," Amy said, brightening. "Sylvia usually sleeps on the pull-out couch in the living room, so you can have that all to yourself instead of sharing the bed with me."

A bus went by as they walked, and on its side was a larger-than-life ad for a TV reality show titled *Model Mania*. "I love that show," Lily remarked to her aunt, happy to change the subject.

"That's the show where girls compete for a modeling contract, isn't it?" Amy asked.

Lily nodded. "You have to be at least seventeen to be on it, though. I'd love to be a model! I hope it's still around when I'm old enough."

"That's five years from now," Amy pointed out.

"Four and a half," Lily corrected her. "Lots of shows stay on that long."

Amy looked Lily over and nodded. "You definitely should model." She spun Lily around so they could both see their images reflected in the store front glass of the dress shop they stood in front of. The curls of Lily's brown hair bounced down her back, and she was almost as tall as her aunt, even though they were almost a decade apart. In the glass, the light of her large brown eyes sparkled back at her.

People were always telling Lily she was pretty. It was flattering to hear, of course, but mostly she didn't give it much importance. But since she'd started watching *Model Mania*, the life of a model had begun to seem exciting to her.

"What do you feel like doing right now?" Amy asked Lily. "It's Saturday and I cleared my schedule so we can do anything you want."

"I don't know," Lily told Amy. "What is there to do around here?"

"Hmm," Amy said, as her forehead crinkled in thought. "We could shop for cool funky jewelry in the East Village, or we could check out Chinatown. If you're up for a hike, it's fun to walk across the Brooklyn Bridge and back. You get a cool view of the East River and you can see the Statue of Liberty out in the harbor."

"That all sounds fun," Lily said. "But it's so hot out today and that sounds like a lot of walking. Is there anything to do nearby?"

"There's a Haunted Museum around the block."

Lily had heard of the Haunted Museum but had never been to one. "I'd love to see that."

"Are you sure it won't give you nightmares?" Amy teased.

Lily rolled her eyes. "I'm sure. Come on. Let's go get haunted!"

• • •

The first thing Lily noticed when she and Amy walked into the main room of the Haunted Museum was all of the DO NOT TOUCH signs posted among the various exhibits.

"Like I would really want to touch any of this creepy stuff," she said quietly to Amy.

"Ah, come on," Amy said. "This place is more cheesy than scary. It's like a cross between the Haunted Mansion at Disneyland, Ripley's Believe It or Not!, and Madame Tussauds wax museum."

Lily saw what Amy meant. Scattered around the room were exhibits that featured life-size replicas of sinister characters. There was a section called Famous Murderers of the Past that made Lily feel as if she were really in the company of Jack the Ripper, Lizzie Borden, and Deacon William Brodie, whom many claim was the inspiration for the character of the murderous Mr. Hyde in Robert Louis Stevenson's *Strange Case of Dr. Jekyll and Mr. Hyde*. There was also a motion-activated talking skeleton dressed like the pirate Long John Silver.

Moving deeper into the museum, Lily saw that different hallways branched off from the main room. Overhead signs identified them. A collection of haunted music boxes, haunted remains from the sunken *Titanic*, and terrifying artifacts of ancient Egypt were among the exhibits. To her right, Lily noticed a hallway leading to an exhibit titled Sinister Portraits.

Lily poked Amy and nodded toward Sinister Portraits. "That sounds cool," she said. "Let's go in there."

A guard dressed in black appeared from out of the shadows. "Don't touch any of the art in there," she snapped.

Lily jumped back, startled by the guard. "No problem," she told the woman. "I wouldn't touch a *thing* in this place — not a single thing."

Amy might think the Haunted Museum was silly, but Lily was starting to feel seriously creeped out.

AMY CHUCKLED softly when they passed a large gold-framed portrait of a man whose eyes moved on their own. "So corny," she commented.

"Yeah, kinda dumb," Lily agreed halfheartedly, but she didn't like the feeling of the painting's eyes still on her as she hurried away from it.

It didn't help that the hall was colder than the main room had been, and darker, too. Little lights below the portraits shone upward, lighting the faces in a way Lily thought was frightening.

Lily let Amy get ahead of her as she lingered over a pastel portrait of Madame Elisabeth, a sister of the French king Louis XVI. The placard next to the portrait said that Madame Elisabeth chose to be beheaded at the guillotine out of loyalty to her brother and his wife, Queen Marie-Antoinette. Madame Elisabeth was said to have haunted her executioner until he went mad and killed himself. Many claimed that only after the man died did her portrait acquire its smug grin.

Lily shivered at the idea. Could it be true?

She moved on to the next portrait painted by an artist named Dimitri Fouquet. It was of Marie Laveau, who some called the Voodoo Queen of New Orleans, with a living rooster in one hand

and a velvet bag in the other. On the table in front of her was a small voodoo doll with nails stuck into it.

Lily felt as though Marie Laveau was gazing right into her heart, and it unsettled her. The next portrait showed Mary, Queen of Scots, being executed. She was blindfolded with arms outstretched beside the executioner, who wore a black leather mask and wielded an ax. The card near the painting claimed that after Mary was beheaded, her lips continued to open and close for fifteen minutes afterward. And when the executioner lifted her head by the hair to show it to the crowd, Mary's head fell out of the wig she wore and rolled through the streets for hours.

Lily folded her arms as a sudden coldness swept over her. What must it be like to have your head cut off? Suddenly she didn't like being alone in the dark hallway. She spied Amy looking at some framed paintings on the wall just ahead and hurried forward to join her.

"Oh, there you are," Amy said when Lily came to her side. "Look at these paintings. What do you think of them?"

Five portraits of girls around Lily's age hung in a perfectly spaced and balanced row. Each of the girls was lovely in her own way, though they seemed to represent different historical eras. Lily read the plaques at the bottom of each portrait.

ROSALIE: CIRCA 1400

ASHLYNNE: CIRCA 1600

ANNE: 1792

EMILY: 1816

JULIA: 1920

Lily turned toward Amy. "What makes these so sinister?"

Amy shrugged but then looked at the card beside the portraits. "It says here that all these paintings were signed by the same artist: Dolores Agonie."

"But that's obviously impossible," Lily said. "They were all painted nearly a hundred years apart."

"That's true," Amy said. "Unless there was a portrait artist who lived to be almost four hundred, the portraits *had* to have been painted by different people."

"They would have to be," Lily agreed.

"And yet . . . ," Amy said, studying the portraits, "the straightforward, almost photographic realism of each painting is alike from portrait to portrait. The artists who did these must have carefully studied the style — the brush strokes, the use of light, the background — of the previous portrait in the series."

"That *is* strange," Lily said as she followed alongside Amy, examining each painting.

"It gets weirder," Amy reported, still reading the card. "These paintings were all found locked away in a trunk covered in chains in an abandoned mansion in Newport, Rhode Island. A sign saying 'Do Not Open for Any Reason' was glued to the trunk."

But why would someone lock these lovely works of art away like that? There must be something really awful about them.

A spell?

A curse?

Lily went from portrait to portrait, studying each girl. Rosalie was a green-eyed redhead in a red gown with a ruffled collar.

Blond, blue-eyed Ashlynne wore a gown of green brocade. A tiny unicorn hung from a golden chain around her neck.

Julia's wavy curls were bobbed to her chin. Her fringed dress clearly evoked the days of the flapper in the 1920s.

Lily stepped backward to view all the portraits together, and realized that all five girls wore the exact same glistening tear-like pearl-drop earrings!

Lily stepped closer to the paintings to inspect them more carefully. She glanced to the right and then the left to see if any guard was nearby, ready to scold her for being too close but she didn't see anyone.

The earrings were somewhat buried in Rosalie's high, thick collar, but they were easy to see under Ashlynne's upswept blond hair. On Anne, the white shimmer of the pearl was harder to find, buried as it was in her light-colored hair.

Lily touched one of the small hoops in her own ears. Mostly she liked hoops and colorful posts, the kinds of earrings she and her friends could find at the mall. How would it feel to wear a set of elegant, glimmering pearls like the ones in the portraits?

Amy came alongside Lily. "What are you staring at?"

"They're all wearing the same earrings," Lily explained. She reached up, pointing to the pearls just below Julia's hair. "See? Even this one. They're buried under her hair but they're right there on the bottom." She brushed the earrings on the painting with her fingertip.

Amy peered at the portraits, taking a closer look, then smiled at Lily. "You're right! And I never would have spotted them on my own. What do you think it means?"

Lily's fingertip tingled where it had brushed the paint and canvas, and she felt a sudden chill run down her spine. "I don't know — they're pretty, though."

What kind of paint was that? Why did it cause that buzz in her hand?

She rubbed her palms together briskly to shake off the weird feeling that had come into her right hand. "I'm starving — do you want to head back home?"

LILY COULDN'T stop thinking about the portraits in the Haunted Museum as she and Amy walked home. Who was this Dolores Agonie? Could the artists all be descendants of the original artist — all with the same name?

"Don't look so serious," Amy said. "I can see that those last five paintings really shook you. They're a joke. A hoax. Did you notice that the signature on each painting was exactly alike?

The same person probably painted them all last year."

Of course Amy was right. "I'm so easy to fool," Lily said, blushing a little. "I always think this kind of stuff could be real."

Amy smiled as she fished in her canvas bag for the keys to her apartment building. "You've got a great imagination. That's all."

"So you don't think they found the portraits locked up in a trunk?" Lily asked.

"No way!" Amy said as she pushed open the door. "I'm sure that was all made up. It's not the Metropolitan Museum of Art! It's the *Haunted Museum!*"

They rode the elevator to the fifth floor and got out at the hall leading to Amy's apartment.

Almost as soon as they turned toward Amy's place, Lily saw that there was a thin, rectangular package leaning against the door. "That's odd,"

Amy said. "Packages usually get left in the down-stairs front hall under the mailboxes."

"Did you order something?" Lily asked.

Amy shook her head and hurried toward her door. Picking up the package, she turned it in her hands, inspecting the brown paper in which it was wrapped. "This was hand-delivered," she told Lily as she handed it over. "And it's for you."

"Me?!" Lily stared at her name written in elegant cursive above Amy's address: Lillian Powers. The return address was to a Daniella Artel.

"Is it from someone you know?" Amy asked as she unlocked the apartment door.

"No."

Lily sat on the couch and unsealed the paper, then opened the top of the brown cardboard box. Sliding out the contents, Lily was amazed. It was the portrait of Julia, the girl from the 1920s, that they'd seen in the Haunted Museum just before.

The girl's dark eyes looked into Lily's, and Lily felt connected to her in some strange way. "How weird," she said quietly.

"That *is* strange," Amy agreed, settling on the couch beside Lily. Picking up the torn wrapping, she checked the return address. "Leonard Street," she read. "This woman lives way downtown on the West Side. Is there any note?"

When Lily upended the empty box, a small envelope fluttered out among the packing peanuts. Lily quickly tore it open:

Dear Lillian,

I was in the Haunted Museum today and saw you admiring my paintings; this one in particular. Should you like to come by someday to see my studio, it would be my pleasure to show you around. No need to call. Stop by anytime. In the meantime please accept this gift from one art lover to another.

Daniella

"Whoa!" Lily shouted excitedly. "How cool is this?!" She held up the letter for Amy to read. "I'd love to meet Daniella," she said to her aunt. "Can we go?"

"Hold on a minute," Amy objected. "I'm not sure I like this. How did she find my apartment? Who told her your real name? Why is she so interested in a total stranger?"

"Uh . . . um . . . ," Lily stammered, trying to come up with answers. "She heard you call me Lily and just figured it was short for Lillian?"

"And my address?" Amy pressed.

Lily's eyes narrowed in thought. "I don't know!" Then she spied a white envelope among the packing materials and bent to pick it up. "It looks like a bill," she said, handing the envelope to Amy.

"How did that get there?" Amy asked. "It was in my bag."

"It must have fallen out."

"I guess that makes sense."

"See?" Lily said. "If she found this on the floor it wouldn't have been too hard to find us. Let's go over there. Please?!"

Amy took her laptop from a shelf and sat on the couch, opening it. Then she slapped the arm of the couch, sighing heavily with frustration. "No Internet! I nearly forgot! I wanted to search for her online. This is the big bad city, kiddo. There are a lot of great people here, but a lot of oddballs, too. You have to be careful."

"I bet she's not an oddball," Lily said. "She's an artist."

"This Daniella could be anyone," Amy went on. "It might not even be a woman. It's best to be careful."

Lily slumped into the couch, disappointed. "I know," she muttered. "It just seemed like it would be such a cool adventure — to meet a famous artist in the city on my first day here. But I guess you're right. We should forget it."

Lily stared at the afternoon sun filtering in through Amy's drawn shade. Outside, the traffic droned steadily, interrupted by intervals of honking horns or emergency sirens. A bead of sweat rolled down her forehead. She noticed electric fans but no air conditioner.

"Oh, cheer up!" Amy said, getting up to turn on a fan. "On Monday I'll check her out while I'm at work and if this woman sounds legit, I'll go over there with you. Okay?"

Amy seemed to be weakening and that encouraged Lily. "Why don't we go to the library tomorrow? They have computers and Internet there, don't they?"

"All right, Little Miss Persistent," Amy agreed. "We'll go tomorrow. And find out who this mysterious Daniella Artel turns out to be."

4

LATER THAT night, after a dinner of order-in pizza and a game of Monopoly that went on for two hours, Amy pulled out the convertible sofa in her small living room and made Lily comfortable with a sheet and pillow. "Want the window open or closed?" Amy asked.

That was a tough question. If the window was shut it would block the horns and traffic and city rumble from outside. But if she left it open, she might catch a breeze — and it was really hot out, even with the fan going. "Open," Lily decided.

Amy said good night and went into her bedroom. Lily sat on the pull-out bed, looking at the painting of Julia. She decided that Julia was someone she would have liked if she'd known her. Julia wasn't exactly smiling — none of the portraits featured smiling girls — but there was a look of merry mischief in her shining eyes. Lily thought she seemed full of fun. Lily could imagine Julia joining her other friends for a slumber party giggling over a prank phone call or rolling with laughter at a downloaded comedy.

With a yawn, Lily leaned the portrait at the side of the couch and pulled up the sheet. Even though she thought the noise from the busy city street would keep her up all night, it wasn't long before she drifted off.

Almost right away, Lily dreamed she was wandering through an apartment building down a long hallway of closed doors. The corridor never turned or ended, but kept going and going. There wasn't any stairway. There was no elevator, not even an exit sign. How did the tenants get to their apartments? How did they leave? The hall seemed never-ending.

Lily knocked on a door. No one answered. She tried door after door. Finally a woman's voice replied warmly, "Who is it?"

"Can you help me?" Lily spoke to the closed door. "How do I get out of here?"

"One moment, dear," the woman behind the door said as she undid the locks on her side.

The door slowly creaked open a crack.

"Oh, thank you so much," Lily spoke with a rush of relief. "I was afraid no one would be home to help —" Lily froze as the door opened fully to reveal a very tall ax-wielding man in an executioner's hood. With a maniacal chortle he lunged from the doorway, his ax high over his head, about to strike.

Lily awoke with a jolt. Her heart hammered frantically and she struggled to breathe. Sweat covered her forehead and cheeks.

"It was a dream," she gasped. "Just a dream."

Lily quickly checked Amy's door, uncertain if she'd cried out in her sleep and awakened her aunt. But Amy's light didn't turn on and Lily was relieved. She was glad she wouldn't have to admit that the Haunted Museum had given her nightmares, after all.

The next time Lily awoke it was still dark, but the first light of dawn had lightened the sky. Why was she awake?

Then she heard it.

Someone was crying.

It was a soft feminine whimpering, hopeless and sad, and its sound brought a lump to Lily's throat. What was making this person so terribly unhappy?

Tossing off her sheet, she crossed the room. "Aunt Amy?" she whispered, tapping lightly on the bedroom door. "Aunt Amy, are you all right?"

When Amy didn't answer, Lily cracked open the door. In the dim light from the streetlamps outside, she saw that Amy slept soundly. Gently shutting the door, Lily listened as the crying continued.

Was it someone in the next apartment? Could the walls be that thin?

Lily put her ear to the one wall that adjoined another apartment. The sound didn't seem to be coming from there. Not from the hallway, either.

But someone *was* crying. Lily could hear the gentle sobs as she sat on her sofa bed to listen intently. Tilting her head to one side, she paid attention to the direction of the crying.

Suddenly she turned to the painting of Julia, still propped up against the side of the bed. The sound of soft sobbing was definitely coming from there.

But how could that be?

With a trembling hand, Lily leaned down to touch the frame. As she lifted it, the crying became louder.

Lily inhaled slowly and her breath caught, too frightened to exhale. This couldn't be real.

Forcing herself to be brave, Lily turned the portrait.

The expression on Julia's face was now twisted in sorrow. In the changed painting, the girl's delicate hand cradled her tear-stained cheek.

Lily dared to touch the painting, only to recoil in surprise. Her fingers were wet!

But not with paint. Lily's fingers had been dampened with Julia's tears.

The sobbing grew louder, more sorrowful.

"Aunt Amy!" Lily shouted. "Come quick!"

There was a rustle as her aunt climbed out of bed and opened the door, and then Amy was beside her. "This painting is crying," Lily told her, pushing the portrait toward her.

Smiling, Amy gave Lily a quick hug. "I told you that place would give you nightmares," she said.

Lily looked at the painting once more. It was completely dry, and Julia had returned to exactly the same position she'd been in when the portrait arrived.

5

On Sunday just after one in the afternoon, Lily and Amy took the subway uptown. They were soon climbing the wide stairs leading to the front of the main branch of the New York City Public Library. On either side of them the library's famous stone lions sat in regal splendor. Normally Lily would have been excited to see them for real, but this afternoon her mind was on other things.

Or one thing: the painting.

"I just wish I'd used my phone to take a picture of Julia," Lily said. "But I was too scared to think of it."

"I wish you had, too," Amy told her. "Then you'd see that there is nothing strange about that painting and you'd stop obsessing about it!"

"I'm not obsessing," Lily insisted, snapping her beaded bracelet with her name spelled out in black and silver beads. That wasn't exactly true — the Julia painting was the *only* thing she'd thought about since the event. But still . . . how could she think of anything else? "And isn't a painting that cries strange? Where else could the sound have come from?"

"Someone in the building had the TV on and was watching a sad movie," Amy suggested.

"Then why were my fingers wet?"

"I don't know. Maybe there's a leak in the ceiling."

When they entered the building, Lily forgot about the crying portrait long enough to marvel at the grandeur of the library, from the high ceilings and rich wood, to the marble floors and staircases. "This is amazing," she whispered. "It's gigantic!"

"It is," Amy agreed while the security guard examined the insides of her bag. "This is one of my favorite places in the city. It's so . . . old."

"And beautiful," Lily added.

Amy knew the library well and easily found her way to a computer. In minutes she was searching the name Daniella Artel.

"Here she is," Amy said as soon as the search engine yielded three results.

The first result was an article about an art gallery exhibit in downtown Manhattan. The work displayed was by portrait artist Daniella Artel. The article gave the time and location, but the show was no longer running.

The second result was a course listing at the Artists Guild in midtown Manhattan. Daniella Artel was teaching a course called "The Power of Portraiture."

The third result was an entry in Wikipedia, the free online encyclopedia. "My language arts teacher won't let us use Wiki," Lily noted. "She says it's unreliable because anyone can write stuff in it."

"I know, my teachers said that, too," Amy replied as she continued to access the website. "But it's still a good jumping-off point, especially the citations at the bottom, and I like to use it, anyway."

Daniella Artel's entry included a photo of a middle-aged woman with blond hair cut to her shoulders. "She was probably pretty when she was younger," Amy remarked.

Lily studied the photo, trying to imagine the lined face without the creases and sagging skin.

Intense blue-gray eyes still sparked under the woman's lids. "Yeah. I bet you're right," Lily said.

"Okay, it says she's an American portrait artist. Date of birth unknown but she's from Arkham, Massachusetts. Studied somewhere in Paris . . . moved to Prague, then to Amsterdam . . . blah, blah, blah."

With Lily peering over her shoulder, Amy hit more keys. She found another site that listed Daniella Artel as a new designer in a famous Parisian fashion house. The date was 1990. The next mention of the woman was when she became an adjunct professor of art at an Italian university in 2005. Still another site contained short biographies of outstanding personalities in contemporary art.

Amy read silently for another minute. "Okay! This is it! Here we go."

"Did you find something good?" Lily asked.

Amy nodded. "Listen to this. Daniella Artel is related to the artist known as Dolores Agonie. Dolores Agonie is thought to be a pseudonym for —"

"A what?"

"A fake name," Amy explained. "Artists and writers sometimes use them."

"Oh. Like Mark Twain's real name was Samuel Clemens?"

"Exactly," Amy confirmed. "So anyway . . . Dolores Agonie is a name used by certain portrait artists through the centuries. They think that all the artists who signed their paintings of young girls with that name were related to each other. It says here that Daniella Artel owns the five existing Dolores Agonie portraits." Amy looked up from her reading. "She must be the person who inherited the collection they found in that attic."

"I thought that the Haunted Museum bought it," Lily said.

"No. It says here that Daniella Artel occasionally lends the portraits to museums and galleries for special showings. She must have loaned them to the Haunted Museum for their Sinister Portraits show."

Amy and Lily stared at each other for a moment. It seemed like they'd uncovered important information, but what did it mean?

"It sounds like Daniella Artel is totally legit," Lily said. *That* was what it meant.

"I guess so," Amy agreed as she exited the website, though she still sounded uncertain.

"So, can we go visit her?"

Amy nodded. "I don't see why not."

"Awesome," Lily said, smiling. "Let's go."

6

THE BUILDING where Daniella Artel lived was so old it had no speaker or bells. And no elevator, either. Checking the mailboxes revealed that D. Artel lived on the sixth floor.

The front lobby was dim, and very quiet. A faded rug was frayed at its edges. Small hexagrams of blue tile on the walls seemed to sweat in the airless heat.

As Lily and Amy ascended the winding

staircase, all the doors were closed. It was as though no one in the building was home. Lily's shoulders tightened as the silent row of closed doors reminded her of her nightmare from the night before.

On the third floor, Amy stopped, panting lightly from the climb. "Could it be any hotter?" she complained.

"I hope not," Lily replied, holding her long hair up off her neck.

On the fifth floor a door was open, revealing a small apartment. Colorful and elaborate print tapestries of varying designs hung on the walls and were draped on the ceiling. The furniture consisted only of some large cushions and a round, low coffee table.

Amy passed it by with hardly a glance, but Lily was fascinated and lingered in front of the doorway.

The smell of some kind of incense and the sound of soft Indian music drifted into the hall from inside the apartment.

Lily saw that cards were spread out on the table. They weren't playing cards, but something else.

A young woman stepped into the room from a back bedroom. Lily guessed that she was still in her late teens. She wore a white tank top and denim shorts. Her short, black curly hair was held back from her face with a bright red head wrap. Her dark eyes brightened when she noticed Lily standing in the hallway. "Hi," she said. "Have you come for a reading?"

"A reading?" Lily asked. "No. What kind of reading?"

The young woman gestured with her hand toward the table. "A tarot card reading? I read palms, too. Is there a spirit you'd like to contact?"

"No. I was just admiring your apartment."

The woman smiled and came to the door. "Nice to meet you. My name's Audreen Santos. I'm a medium, a spirit channeler."

"Hi, I'm —" Lily began to introduce herself.

Audreen cut Lily short with a raised palm. "Let me guess."

"All right."

"Your name is a flower."

"Yes!"

"A lily."

"Wow! Yeah! How did you ever guess that?"

Audreen Santos smiled lightly. "Lilies are flowers sent when people die."

Lily didn't like the sound of that.

Audreen suddenly gripped her arm. "In fact, I see spirits of the dead around you right now. You must be very careful."

Despite the heat, Lily felt a sudden coldness wash over her.

"Spirits of the dead?" Lily asked fearfully.

Audreen's face was serious as she nodded. "Ghosts."

Spirits? Ghosts? Around her? "Why are they around me?" Lily asked.

Audreen squinted with concentration, tilting her head. "I don't know. They want to talk to you, not to me."

Prickles of fear crept up Lily's spine. "I don't want to talk to them."

"They might have something urgent to tell you."

"Like what?"

"Come inside and I'll try to connect you with them," Audreen offered.

"Lily, come on!" Amy called from up ahead. "Where are you?"

"I'm coming!" Lily shouted back.

"But the spirits," Audreen reminded Lily.

"I'm sorry," Lily said, backing away from the

door. "My aunt's calling. I have to go. It was nice meeting you."

"You, too," Audreen replied. "Be careful, okay?"

"Careful of what?"

"That's what I want to ask the spirits. Are you sure you can't stay?"

"Lily! Come on!" Amy called again.

"Bye," Lily said to Audreen. "I'll come by when we're done. Would that be all right?"

"I'll be here, definitely! I think it's important."

"Okay. I will."

"Lily!" Amy's voice was sharp and insistent.

"Sorry! I'm coming." Lily encountered Amy as she was walking back down the staircase toward her. "You won't believe what just happened to me," she told Amy.

"What happened? Are you all right?"

"I'm fine. But listen to this." She told Amy about Audreen and about being surrounded by the dead.

"Yeah, right," Amy said, lifting an eyebrow. "New York City is full of people claiming to be psychics and fortune-tellers and all. They're fakes."

"Audreen isn't a fake," Lily insisted "She knew my name without my telling her."

Amy coughed and glanced meaningfully down at Lily's beaded bracelet. Feeling foolish, Lily lifted her wrist and looked at the letters *L-I-L-Y* strung on the elastic cord. "I forgot I was wearing this."

"See what I mean? These people are clever."

At the top of the stairs, they stopped outside an apartment with the name D. ARTEL printed on a label on the door. Amy rapped on the door and Lily sucked in her breath. Even though Daniella Artel had invited them, Lily suddenly felt anxious about dropping in on her without emailing or calling.

"One moment," a melodic female voice called from inside the apartment. There was movement at the small peephole and then the door opened.

A tall, delicate blond woman in her forties appeared, wearing a white blouse and lightweight black pants. Her gleaming hair was swept up in a loose knot at the back of her head, and vivid blue-gray eyes shone warmly out at them. "Lillian!" she cried with delight. "I thought you'd never get here."

7

D ANIELLA INVITED Amy and Lily inside. "Welcome! Welcome!"

Lily had never seen an apartment like the one that belonged to Daniella Artel. The sun shone into the wide open space. The kitchen was on one side of the large room, and a canopy-covered bed peeked over a woven screen on the opposite wall. A wooden floor gleamed with high polish and a gold chandelier festooned in shimmering prismatic crystals hung from the fifteen-foot ceiling, throwing rainbows of light around the room.

The place was filled with artwork of every kind. Framed photos in black and white, as well as in color, depicting people of many ages and ethnicities covered the walls. Lily thought she recognized celebrities, models, even designers in some of them. Paintings and frames leaned against a wall under a window, out of the sunlight. A modern multicolored glass spiral stood beside a realistic-looking clay sculpture of a girl, and Amy took a step toward them as she looked intently at the two very different sculptures.

"Those two pieces have more in common than you might think," Daniella commented from the kitchen area, where she was pouring three glasses of lemonade. "One shows the outside of the girl, while the other depicts the many colors of her inner being and her spirit spiraling to the sky. That's why I always display them together."

"I see what you mean," Amy said.

Lily glanced back and forth between the two sculptures. "But why is her spirit spiraling upward? Shouldn't it be inside her?"

Daniella seemed to study Lily for a long moment before speaking. "Energy moves through our bodies and all around us," Daniella said. "To capture what can't be seen is as much an artist's challenge as is replicating what can be seen."

"Cool," Lily said, studying the Plexiglas spiral.

The word *cool* made Lily realize that Daniella's apartment was, in fact, very cold, and she shivered.

"Would you like me to turn down the air-conditioning?" Daniella offered.

Lily was about to say yes, but Amy jumped in ahead of her. "Absolutely not! We've been baking in the heat all day. This is like heaven!"

"It's expensive to keep the apartment this cold but my art materials don't work as well in the scorching heat."

Gazing around, Lily saw several fancy cameras on Daniella's large work table. Beside them were silk screen print equipment, a collection of chalk pastels, and a palette crowded with oil paints. An artist's easel was set up in a corner of the room. On it was a half-finished painting of a girl about Lily's age.

Something in the girl's expression caught Lily's interest. It was familiar somehow. Lily crossed the room to the painting to see it better.

The portrait was definitely in the style of the ones done by the Dolores Agonie artists. This girl was too unfinished to tell what era she belonged

to, but her green eyes were beautiful and clear —
though Lily couldn't help but feel they looked
nervous.

"Do you like it?" Daniella asked.

Lily wasn't sure if *like* was the right word.
"Will this be another portrait in the collection
from Dolores Agonie?" she asked.

"Are you one of her relatives?" Amy put in
before Daniella could answer.

"Yes and yes," Daniella answered as she set the
glasses of lemonade on the table. "The last of
the portraits was painted by my grandmother.
It's high time I do another one."

"We read that the other ones got locked in an
attic," Amy said.

Daniella rolled her eyes. "My ex-husband was
a bit of an eccentric," she said. "I inherited the
paintings when my mother passed on, and they'd
always bothered him. So one day he packed them

up and hid them away in a New England barn before continuing his trip up to Canada."

"You must have been furious with him when he came home," Amy commented.

"He never did come home," Daniella said.

"Oh, I'm sorry," Amy said, looking embarrassed.

"Not at all." Daniella waved away the idea of any remorse over her husband's disappearance. "I was relieved, really. But it took me years to track down the paintings. Years!"

"Why did you send one of them to me?" Lily asked.

"You seemed to be so fascinated by it at the Haunted Museum," Daniella said. "You and the girl in the portrait share the same kind of energy, and I thought you belonged together."

"You were at the museum?" Lily asked.

"Yes. I like to stay in the shadows and observe

the reactions people have to the portraits. Lily, when I saw you I was struck by your appreciation for the portraits and by your beauty."

"Isn't she pretty?" Amy agreed.

"No," Daniella said, "not pretty — beautiful. Those high cheek bones! The arched brow! The long neck! A beauty like Lily comes along only once a century."

"Wow!" Lily said, feeling self-conscious. "Thanks." No one had ever been *this* complimentary about her appearance before.

"Have you ever thought of modeling?" Daniella asked Lily.

"I *have* thought about it," Lily replied. "I've been watching that show about models in New York City — I'd love to be on it when I'm old enough, if I can."

"Why wait? I can start your career," Daniella said. "I've been hired to take photos for — well, it hasn't been announced yet — for a national chain of stores. They're opening a new line of teen fashions with my dear friend Manolo von Maheim, and they want one girl to represent the line. It's called International Spirit."

Lily's heart began to race. She'd heard of models and actresses being discovered in schools and malls, but never thought it would actually happen to her.

"The shoot would be in August, and you would be paid of course," Daniella went on. "But there is one condition."

"What's that?" Amy asked in that skeptical tone Lily was coming to dread.

"I have to be certain that Lily can model."

"I'm sure she can," Amy said. "How hard can it be?"

Lily thought of the episodes she'd seen of *Model Mania*. It didn't look like modeling was as simple as Amy thought. The girls on the show were always being directed not to be so stiff, and to have good posture, and not to pout, and to *smile* with their eyes.

"Do you think you can model, Lily?" Daniella asked.

"I think so — but I've never done it before," Lily admitted.

"Exactly," Daniella said. "So how about this. You'll come here and sit for one of my portraits. You'll get some training, I'll give you some tips, and we'll see how it goes. Naturally, I will pay you for sitting, too."

Lily turned to Amy, smiling and excited. "I can do it, can't I?"

"We'll have to call your mom. But I don't see why she'd object."

Lily could come up with lots of reasons why her cautious mother would object, but she didn't want to think about them. This was the beginning of the career in modeling that she'd dreamed of! Working with Daniella would be great. She was so sophisticated and creative, and Lily was already determined to impress her. She couldn't wait to get started.

They talked some more about the times they would work and when Lily would get paid. Daniella told her to wear a plain outfit and to leave her hair loose. "And no makeup! I want to capture that unspoiled beauty."

Finally Daniella rose from the couch saying she had to get ready for an appointment. "So I'll see you tomorrow?" she asked.

"I'll be here," Lily assured her. She glanced at the half-finished painting on the easel. "Will a day be enough time for you to finish that other painting over there?"

"Oh, I'm not going to complete that one. I'll start fresh with you."

"But it's so lovely," Amy objected. "Why not complete it?"

"I lost my model."

"What happened to her?" Lily asked.

Daniella looked away. "I don't know. She never came back."

8

LILY WAS so excited about modeling that she practically floated back home. They stopped to pick up Chinese food on the way, talking about Daniella and her studio as they walked.

Once they got back to Amy's apartment, they set their bags down on the coffee table and Lily breathed in the ginger aroma that rose from the hot food. The spicy scent reminded her of something she'd meant to do. . . .

"I forgot!" Lily exclaimed, and Amy glanced at her over her shoulder as she reached into the kitchen cabinets for plates and forks. "I told Audreen I would come by on our way down the stairs."

"Why bother?" Amy asked as she helped Lily unload the white cardboard cartons. "You don't honestly think you're surrounded by the dead, do you?"

"I guess not," Lily replied. Of course the idea was crazy. But still . . . "She was nice, though," Lily added, "and I did say I would come."

"All those psychic people are nice at the start. They want you to pay them to read your palm."

"She said she reads tarot cards, and all kinds of things."

Amy began to spoon food onto her plate. "Well, stay away from her. You don't want to spend all the money you're going to make modeling on that kind of thing." Amy took a deep breath and smiled. "It was nice of your mom to give me some money to help pay for your food and stuff. Normally I'd be eating ramen noodles tonight."

"I like ramen noodles," Lily said.

"Yeah, but not every night," Amy said as she began to eat her eggplant with garlic ginger sauce.

"It's so exciting, isn't it?" Lily said, scooping some beef and broccoli from a container. "Me! A model!"

"It is, but it's too bad you have to sit for that portrait before you pose for the photo spread," Amy said.

"I don't mind. I think the portraits are cool." Lily crossed the room to the portrait of Julia that she'd propped up on a side table so that the picture was supported by the wall. "And I don't mind being in one of the portraits — the girl in this one is so pretty, isn't she?" Lily said to Amy.

Amy looked up from the food and nodded. "She *is* pretty. All the girls in the portraits are."

Lily touched her earlobes. "It's a good thing I got my ears pierced. I hope I'll get to wear a pair of earrings like all the girls in the portraits have on."

"Remind me to call your mother," Amy said. "We need her permission before you can do it."

"Okay," Lily agreed. Amy hadn't said anything more about Lily having to stay so close to the apartment while Amy worked. Posing for Daniella would be much more interesting than being cooped up all day. Lily's hopes about spending the summer in the city were turning out better than she'd imagined.

The afternoon was still sweltering and Amy's electric fans were no match for it. "Would you mind if I took a nap?" Amy asked. "We can go out again once the sun sets."

"No problem," Lily agreed. The food and the heat had made her drowsy, too. She set up the couch bed and stretched out on top of it.

The person in the apartment next door was playing a record, sort of an old-time jazz tune, lively and happy. Lily yawned, turning onto her side. The fan at the window blew Amy's gauzy white curtains while the music blended in with the traffic noises from the street.

Soon Lily drifted into a dream where she floated out into the street, flying over the buildings. She often dreamed that she could fly, but it was always over trees and yards. She'd never had an airborne city dream like this.

Then Lily's eyes fluttered open and she was back on the pull-out bed. The delicate curtains still fluttered but now they seemed to be making noise.

Lily propped herself onto one elbow, leaning forward so she could hear better.

"Lily! Lily!" The voice was whisper-soft and lilting, pleasant. "Lily! Lily!"

Lily glanced at her aunt's closed bedroom door. The voice wasn't coming from that direction, and besides, it wasn't Amy's usual tone.

No, it seemed as though the billowing curtains were calling her.

But how could that be?

Was she mistaking the whir of the fan for words?

"Lily, I have to show you something."

Lily sat up straight on the edge of the couch. Those last words were definitely not made by the fan blades. "Who's there?" Lily whispered.

Behind the curtains, a figure began to take form. It was a girl with dark curls to her chin. Her gauzy dress blew along with the curtains, making her even harder to see.

"Who — are you?" Lily asked as she slid from the bed to stand.

"I'm Julia," said the figure.

She looked like the portrait, but the girl in the

picture had coffee-colored skin and pretty brown eyes. This girl's skin was chalk white. Her eyes were completely black, with no color in them at all.

Lily hugged herself, suddenly freezing.

"Come with me, Lily. I have to show you something."

The ghostly Julia stood in the open window, the sunset glowing orange behind her.

Lily crept toward the window until she and this otherworldly figure stood an arm's length apart. "What do you want to show me?" Lily asked.

Julia beckoned, waving Lily closer. She floated from the window, hovering in the air. "Come with me."

Lily knew it made no sense, but somehow she trusted Julia.

She reached out, extending her hand, sure that Julia would grasp it and keep her from falling.

L ILY!" A MY shrieked.

Amy's voice jolted Lily, as though someone had just shaken her awake from a dream.

Where had Julia gone?

Amy clamped both her hands on Lily's shoulders and pulled her back toward the center of the room. "You looked like you were about to jump out the window. What were you doing?!"

Lily looked at Amy but she couldn't reply. She wasn't exactly sure what to say. It would have been insane to step off the window ledge, but she'd been so certain that Julia wouldn't let her fall.

"Are you even awake?" Amy asked.

She was, but she let Amy steer her back to the pull-out bed, still feeling too stunned and dazed to speak.

Amy wrapped her arms around Lily. "Why didn't you or your mom tell me you're a sleepwalker?"

But Lily had never walked in her sleep. Not ever! She gripped Amy's arm. How could she have done such a thing? She would have stepped out if Amy hadn't stopped her.

Was it the heat? Could she be losing her mind?

When Lily looked at Amy again, her aunt was crying. "What if you had fallen? You never would have survived."

"But I didn't fall. I'm fine," Lily said, finding her voice once more. "And I've never —"

Amy went to the window, slamming it shut and turning the latch. Sweat beaded on Lily's forehead and the heat made her feel faint. "No, please don't do that. Nothing else will happen. I've never walked in my sleep before."

"I don't care if we melt into puddles," Amy replied. "I'm not opening that window."

"We'll die in this heat," Lily protested.

"You'll *die* if you fall out the window!" Amy shouted, throwing her arms wide. "Come on, let's go. I'm buying an air conditioner. I'll take out another credit card if I have to."

•   •   •

Every store Amy and Lily went to was sold out of air conditioners. "We can order you one but it won't come in for a week," was all they heard.

When they returned to the apartment, it was sweltering. "Please open the window," Lily pleaded.

"All right," Amy gave in and pushed the window sash up. "But I'm not taking my eyes off of you."

"You don't have to watch me."

"Yes, I do."

"I'm not asleep, so I'm not going to sleep walk," Lily argued.

"I don't care."

That night Amy called Lily's mother and told her about the modeling job. Lily could barely breathe, trying to imagine what her mother was saying.

"Yes, I'll bring her there and pick her up every time," Amy said. "Daniella seems very nice, and she has an impressive portfolio. . . ." Lily's mother wasn't easily convinced, and Lily began to think her big modeling opportunity would be over before it began. But finally Amy put down the phone and smiled. "Okay, you're on for tomorrow."

Jumping from her chair, Lily hugged Amy. "Thank you for talking her into it. I know it wasn't easy."

"You've got to have your cell phone charged and on every minute."

"I will."

"And I'm going to drop you off in the morning."

"Okay."

"And you can't go out without letting me know."

"I won't."

"And for goodness sake — no more sleep-walking!"

"I won't!" Lily said. "I promise. Thank you for not telling Mom."

"I didn't want to scare her or make her come get you," Amy said. "What was going on in your head? Were you dreaming?"

"I guess so," Lily replied. She glanced at the portrait of Julia on the dresser. It looked exactly as it had when she received it.

Or did it?

Had there always been that hint of concern in the girl's eyes?

"I was dreaming about the portrait," Lily said. "Amy, does it look any different to you than it did before?"

Amy studied the painting quickly and then shook her head. "No. Does it look different to you?"

"No," Lily said quickly, but she wasn't sure.

. . .

That night, Amy slept with Lily on the pull-out bed. "I'm tying this string between my ankle and yours," Amy said as she unwound a ball of yarn. "You won't be able to get up without me knowing about it."

"We're going to get tangled up," Lily objected.

"I don't move much once I'm asleep," Amy replied firmly. "It'll be fine."

Almost as soon as she turned out the lamp, Amy was snoring lightly. Lily lay beside her, eyes wide open, thinking of the day's events. Tomorrow she'd start modeling. It was so exciting!

An unexpected cool breeze wafted in the window and drew Lily's attention to the fluttering curtains, lit by the streetlamp outside the window. She'd been trying not to look at them because they drew her eye out the window. And she didn't want to think about that because it scared her. She had almost jumped out the window. But why?

Lily glanced once more at the portrait of Julia. She could see that new worried look in the eyes. Lily blinked hard, trying to return the girl's expression to what it had been. This had to be a trick of the fan blades scattering the streetlight's glow around the room.

Lily shut her eyes and then checked again. Julia's painted eyes bore into her. Dark circles had begun to form underneath them. The edges of her mouth drooped, and lines formed across her forehead.

It's melting. That had to be the answer. The paint was sliding down off the canvas. Daniella had said her art materials didn't do well in the heat, but Lily had never imagined this.

Lily turned to shake Amy awake — she had to see this — but Amy only sputtered and turned to her side.

When Lily glanced back at the painting, Julia's black hair had become streaked with wide bands of gray.

And then the frame began to move, growing and expanding until the figure inside was life-size.

Lily clutched Amy's arm, terrified, as Julia began to rise. Her gnarled, veiny hands clutched the sides of the frame, pulling herself forward.

A shriek of terror froze in Lily's throat. She was too shocked to make a sound.

Julia continued rising, climbing out of the frame until she was kneeling on the dresser. Her long white hair danced around her haggard face, tossed by the fan. Her lacy white dress was now so old and shredded that she seemed to be clothed in cobwebs.

Spreading her arms wide, the ancient figure rose from the dresser and floated to the middle of the room, hovering above Lily.

Lily trembled as any icy cold enveloped her, her teeth clacking together violently.

The haggish figure gazed down at Lily and grinned. Rotted teeth began to fall onto Lily, hundreds of them, as if it were raining teeth.

Shielding herself with her arm, Lily was deafened by the sound of her own screams.

10

THE NEXT thing Lily knew, she was surrounded by light. It blinded her.

"Are you all right, Lily?" Amy was on the floor beside her, their ankles still tied.

Where was the floating figure? The teeth? What was happening?

"Why are we on the floor?" Lily asked.

"You screamed, fell out of bed, and dragged me with you." Amy pushed her bright red hair out of her eyes. "That must have been some dream you had."

Lily quickly stood, looking around the room. The portrait of Julia sat on the dresser, returned to its normal size. She was nearly smiling, and her expression had returned to the way it was when Lily had first opened the package. Almost. That hint of worry still played in her eyes.

"Do you want to talk about it?" Amy asked, untying the string that connected them.

"It wasn't a dream," Lily said, pointing to the portrait. "Amy, she grew old right in front of me, and climbed out of the frame."

"Out of the picture frame?" Amy asked doubtfully.

"Yes!" Lily said. "She floated in the air, and her rotten teeth were falling out. But there were so many teeth!"

Amy bent to pick something off the floor. "Do

you mean a tooth like this?" she asked, holding up a brownish, pronged tooth.

"Yes!" Lily shouted, cringing back in horror. "Do you see? It was real."

Amy shook her head and smiled gently. "Sorry, hon. My cat, Jinx, died just last week. She was twenty, which is ancient for a cat. At the end she was losing teeth like crazy. I've vacuumed a ton of them, but I'm still finding them around."

Lily stared at the pointed tooth, unconvinced.

"It really happened, Aunt Amy," she said. "At first I thought the paint was melting but then I saw she was growing older — right in front of me!"

"You had a nightmare, kiddo. It happens," Amy said. "I think you must have seen some of these teeth lying around and they worked themselves into your dream, like the fan did the other night when you thought you heard crying."

"No," Lily sputtered, dismayed. "These things are really happening. They're not like dreams at all."

"I know one thing," Amy said, getting up and sitting on the bed. "Tomorrow when we go to Daniella's place, we're returning that portrait to her. It's giving you nightmares."

"But we'll insult her if we do that," Lily said.

"She'd probably want it back rather than have me throw it in the trash — because that's where I'm putting it if she doesn't take it back."

"All right. Okay," Lily agreed. Even though the portrait was frightening, she couldn't bear the idea of something so beautiful being thrown away.

Amy went to the recycling pile out in the hall near the garbage chute and came back with a pile of last week's newspapers. She used them to wrap the portrait, tying it up with the yarn she'd used to connect their ankles. "There," she said, satisfied. "In the morning this is out of here."

Amy retied their ankles before shutting off the light to go back to sleep. "Sweet dreams this time," she said to Lily as she made herself comfortable on the pillow.

"Thanks. You, too."

But even though Lily tried to sleep, her mind raced. She remembered the sorrowful sobbing and pictured the lovely, young Julia floating out the window, leached of all color except for the orange light of the sunset behind her. The images of the paint melting down the canvas, the rapid aging Julia had undergone, and the terrible rain of rotting teeth played again and again in her mind.

Lily's imagination had never played tricks on her like this before. So why was it happening now?

At eight the next morning, Amy and Lily were on the subway headed for Daniella's apartment. Lily clutched the overhead bar as the tightly packed crowd swayed in unison every time the subway car went around a curve. The air conditioner blasted at full roar but the crush of commuting bodies overpowered it, making Lily feel almost dizzy with heat.

"Welcome to rush hour on the subway," Amy said with a smile, placing her hand on Lily's back.

"Why are so many people dressed in black in this heat?" Lily asked. Back home, pastels and bright colors were more common summer wear.

"Black is New York chic," Amy replied. She pointed to her own black cotton shirt.

Lily suddenly felt out of place in her orange T-shirt and denim shorts. Amy caught her expression and smiled. "Don't worry. Not *everyone* wears black."

Looking around, Lily saw that there was still a mix of colors despite the multitude of black.

With a squeal of brakes, the subway stopped and the doors whooshed open. "This is our stop, kiddo," Amy told her.

When they came up from the subway onto the sidewalk, Amy tucked the wrapped portrait of Julia under her arm.

They walked, and Lily looked around, watching the city come to life — so many people already heading to work. The traffic was heavy on the streets. The crowds walking in both directions forced Lily and Amy to bob and weave through them.

Lily wondered if she would move to Manhattan if she became a model. She'd probably have to, and she decided that was fine. Despite the constant noise and the crowds, she liked it here. The activity and excitement of it all appealed to her.

"This has really worked out great, hasn't it?" Amy said. "Now you have something interesting to do while I'm at work. You don't have to be cooped up in my apartment all alone. Plus, Daniella keeps her air-conditioning at full blast. What could be better than that?"

Lily hoped Audreen Santos would be home and could see her. Well, sort of. The idea of talking about the spirit world had tied her stomach into a knot. But the thought of falling out a window or having more terrifying dreams was worse, and this was the only hope she had of understanding what was happening.

"Come on, Lily, smile," Amy urged. "Everything is going to be fine."

Lily forced a fake smile but then relaxed into a real one. Amy was right. It would be fine. Modeling for Daniella Artel was a once-in-a-lifetime opportunity. She should be happy, not worried.

They turned right onto Leonard Street and found Daniella's apartment. "Good luck today, Lily," Amy said.

"Thanks." Lily headed to the front door and pushed it open with a wave to her aunt. Then she abruptly turned back. "I almost forgot the painting."

"Oh! Right! The . . ." Amy looked all around

but she had no painting. "Where could it have gone?" she remarked. "I was sure I had it."

"You did. It was under your arm," Lily said. "What happened?"

"This is impossible. How could it just disappear?" Amy said.

"It must have slipped out from under your arm."

Amy and Lily retraced their path back to the subway station. "I know I had it when we came above ground," Amy recalled.

They checked in corners, near trash bins, and under cars parked on the street, but the painting wasn't there. Lily and Amy stared at each other, both of them baffled.

"I guess we wanted to get rid of the painting anyway," Amy said.

"What if someone finds it and returns it to Daniella?" Lily asked, worried.

"Let's hope that doesn't happen."

Lily nodded. That would definitely be awkward.

"We'd better get going," Amy told Lily.

With a nod, Lily waved good-bye to Amy again as she descended down the subway stairs.

Lily walked back to Daniella's apartment and was in front of the building when her phone buzzed inside her bag. Lily took it out and clicked the message icon.

Instead of opening a message from Amy like she'd expected, a video came on.

It was video from the night before. The ancient hag Julia floated in the air. She screamed, and teeth flew from her mouth. There were hundreds of teeth, brown and rotten and impossible, more teeth than one human could possibly have. Lily held the phone at arm's length, as far from her eyes as she possibly could.

But under the terrible scream, Lily heard the spirit saying something — or attempting to speak, anyway. Her words were a garbled roar.

Lily held the phone closer to her ear, listening. It sounded as though several people were talking at once, and their words overlapped so that there was no way for them to be heard clearly.

Why hadn't she noticed the voices last night? Probably because she'd been too terrified by what she was seeing.

Lily's hand shook but she didn't want to drop her phone. This was her proof. She hadn't imagined anything.

But who could have taken this?

Who had sent it?

Her hand was trembling so hard that Lily couldn't read the name of the sender when she tried to check it.

Finally she steadied herself enough to see what the phone said.

Nothing! There was no sender.

Lily stood on the sidewalk, her heart racing.

"Are you ready to start working?"

Startled by the unexpected voice, Lily yelped and jumped back. Daniella Artel stood in the shade of her apartment building, holding the door open. "Daniella, you scared me!"

"Sorry, dear," Daniella apologized. Her blond hair was tied back in a colorful silk scarf and she wore a plain white sundress. "You seem distressed. Is everything all right?"

"I . . . I just got a very strange video from someone," Lily replied. "It was a text message, but with no sender!"

"I don't understand," Daniella said. "These new gadgets are a mystery to me; I don't have a cellular phone."

"Here, I'll show you," Lily said.

But she wasn't quite sure how to get back to the video. She checked her video app, but the last thing there was a video of the spring play at school. Maybe it was in a text message?

Lily hesitated. Did she really want to see this again?

Yes — she did. She needed to show someone.

Lily checked her texts and saw that the most recent message had come from a number marked 000000. "Here. Look at this," Lily said, hitting the number and handing the phone to Daniella.

A horrendous shrieking blasted from the phone.

Daniella cringed away, stumbling backward, dropping the phone on the sidewalk and covering her ears.

Lily jumped, too. The scream was making her ears hurt.

"Make it stop!" Daniella cried.

Lily bent for the phone and saw only white static crackling on the screen. But something about the screaming was familiar.

She was reaching for the phone when she realized where she'd heard that screaming before.

It was her own voice.

12

LILY SAT on a high stool with her long hair fanned around her shoulders, one side tucked behind her ear. Daniella moved a screen to bounce some light toward Lily, then stepped back to study her. "You wore a T-shirt and shorts, very good," she said. "But it's too plain by itself. What else should you wear?"

"Some kind of sweater?" Lily suggested. "I'm kind of cold."

Daniella crossed the room to a large black trunk and lifted the lid. It was full of colorful folds of fabric, which Daniella rummaged through before withdrawing a purple-and-blue, paisley-print shawl. "This could be striking with your dark hair and eyes," she remarked. "Let's try it."

As she draped it around Lily's shoulders, Lily cast an anxious glance at her bag, where she'd stowed her phone. What would she find the next time she looked at it?

"Worried about your phone?" Daniella asked.

Lily nodded, remembering the awful screaming.

"I'm sure it was simply a malfunction," Daniella said. "That wasn't a scream. I've heard audio equipment make a similar high-pitched sound when it starts to go bad. They probably have to fix a wire or some such nuisance."

But where could the video have come from?

"You won't have to worry about your phone while you're with me," Daniella added, still fussing with the scarf. "I don't have any computers here."

"Why not?" Lily asked.

"I hate the things. They confuse me. It took me long enough to get used to the telephone."

Lily looked at the old rotary-style phone on Daniella's table. "Didn't you grow up using a phone?" Lily asked. Daniella wasn't a very young woman but she wasn't ancient, either.

"I grew up on a farm," Daniella said, stepping back. Something dark and guarded in her tone gave Lily the impression that this wasn't a happy memory. "We didn't have many modern conveniences."

"Was that in Arkham, Massachusetts?" Lily asked.

Daniella stared at her sharply. "How do you know that?"

Lily regretted having spoken. Clearly Daniella wasn't happy.

"I read it."

"Where?" Daniella demanded.

"Online. After you sent Julia's portrait, Aunt Amy and I wanted to know more about you, so we Googled you. You're in Wikipedia."

"You what? I'm in what?"

"Wikipedia. It's an online encyclopedia."

"These are all computer things I assume," Daniella said, her distress diminishing. "You say there's information about me available through a computer? Who would have put it there?"

"I don't know. Anyone can enter things into the Wikipedia website."

"Web? Oh, never mind," Daniella said with a dismissive wave of her hand. "The invasion of my privacy disturbs me deeply, though. There was a time when one could bury one's past in the past."

"Why would . . . *one* . . . want to do that?" Lily asked. "It sounds to me like you've had a very interesting life."

"Yes. But my life is my business."

"I suppose so," Lily agreed. She'd never experienced a world where there was no Internet — how hard must it have been to find anything without Google?

"No matter," Daniella said, brightening. "There's nothing computerish here, so your pesky phone can't bother you."

"You don't have any Wi-Fi?" Lily asked.

"Whatever that is — I assure you I don't have it."

Lily had promised to keep her cell phone on. Her mother had only allowed her to do this on the condition that she was available by phone the whole time. "Well, as long as there's cell service, my mom or Aunt Amy can call if they need to."

"I have no idea what any of that means. But without such interruptions we will work quite undisturbed." Folding her arms, she assessed Lily critically. "I know what your look requires. I have exactly the thing. I'll be right back."

Daniella glided over to her dresser behind the screen and returned holding a small box. "Here!" she said, smiling as she opened it. "This will be just the right touch."

Nestled on a burgundy velvet cushion inside was a pair of elegant pearl-drop earrings. "Just like in the paintings," Lily said softly, awed to see the earrings for real. "They're so beautiful." Up close, the pearls had a pink tint and were larger than Lily had expected. "I noticed them in the portraits on display in the Haunted Museum. Every girl wore the same earrings."

"Very observant," Daniella said. "They've been handed down in my family for centuries. The pearls are originally from the bottom of the Dead Sea."

"I thought nothing could live in the Dead Sea," Lily said. "It's too salty. That's why they call it *dead*."

"Yes, some call it the Sea of Death. The bottom of the Dead Sea is one of the lowest places on earth. There's a theory that there are underwater springs now, but people used to believe it was an opening to the underworld."

"So how could pearls form inside of oysters there?"

Daniella turned the box of pearl earrings lovingly in her hands. "No one knew. There's an old family legend that they were originally a gift given to an Egyptian princess by a demon who rose from the deep underwater trench of the Dead Sea."

"Wow!" Lily murmured. The earrings began emitting a pink glow that washed over Daniella's face, making her appear especially beautiful.

"What happened?" Lily asked, intrigued by the tale.

"Are you sure you want to hear this?" Daniella asked. "It's a bit disturbing."

"I'm sure," Lily said. "Tell me, please."

Daniella sat on her high artist's stool and inhaled deeply. "All right, if you insist. I'll tell you."

13

"THIS IS the story that is told of these very pearl earrings," Daniella began. "The demon from the bottom of the Dead Sea attempted to bewitch the princess into thinking she loved him in return, even though he was hideous to look at and oozed pure evil. At first she resisted, but then he gave her these earrings."

"And that won her over?" Lily guessed.

Daniella nodded. "The princess was dazzled by the beauty of the earrings and couldn't resist trying them on. The bedeviled earrings made the princess think the demon was the most charming, radiant man she had ever seen. This broke the heart of the young prince whom she had loved before, and who still loved her desperately."

"What happened?" Lily asked, fascinated.

"Enchanted, the princess willingly followed the demon back to the Dead Sea, where he intended to take her back to the underworld with him. But the prince secretly followed. He had been spying on the demon and the princess and suspected that the pearls were at the heart of the enchantment."

"He was right about that!" Lily exclaimed.

"Yes, he was and just when the princess was about to enter the water with the demon, the prince grabbed her and unhooked the pearl earrings."

"A happy ending!" Lily cried in delight.

Daniella shook her head sadly. "The demon was much stronger than the prince and grabbed the princess, quickly dragging her below to the underwater trench, which was the gateway to his underworld kingdom. The prince dove in after her and was drowned."

"How could he drown?" Lily asked. "It's so salty there. Wouldn't he float?"

"It's a myth that you can't drown in the Dead Sea. People are poisoned by the salty water if they swallow too much of it. As they're choking, they can't push off the bottom to save themselves because it's too deep."

"If the earrings were lost in the Dead Sea, how did your family get them?"

"Back in the eleventh century during the first Crusade, a peasant was collecting mud from the Dead Sea to sell. Even then people believed it had healing properties. He found the earrings in the mud and quickly sold them to the powerful order of English knights fighting in the Middle East known as the Knights Templar."

"And your family got them from the Knights Templar?"

"In a way," Daniella answered.

"What do you mean?"

Daniella looked away, her expression suddenly uncomfortable. "In the fourteenth century, the knights were arrested or killed, and their fortunes were stolen. The earrings fell into the hands of the Borgia family who dominated much of Rome in the late Middle Ages. I am a direct descendant of Lucrezia Borgia. The earrings have been passed down from her. It's even rumored that she secretly did the first portrait in the Dolores Agonie series."

Daniella handed the earrings to Lily. "Put them on, dear."

Gazing down at the earrings, Lily hesitated. They shimmered with some inner light, and she imagined that when she wore them she'd also look like the girls in the portraits. They were truly dazzling. For some reason, though, she didn't want to put them on.

"What's wrong?" Daniella asked.

Lily wasn't really sure, but felt foolish admitting that.

"They're so expensive. I'm afraid I'll break them." It was all she could think of.

"Nonsense," Daniella said. "How can you possibly hurt them? I won't let you leave here still wearing them, you can be certain of that."

"They feel heavy," Lily said. "They might tear my ear."

"Now you're just being juvenile," Daniella said with an edge of annoyance in her voice. "Women have worn them for centuries. I've worn them myself. Do you want the honor of being the subject of a genuine Dolores Agonie portrait or do you not?"

Lily wasn't so sure she did want this honor — not after she'd seen the terrifying thing her portrait of Julia was capable of. Did she really want to see her face hanging in the Sinister Portraits collection in the Haunted Museum?

What Lily absolutely did want, however, was the modeling contract that would come afterward. That was the prize, which would make all this worthwhile.

"I do," Lily said. She slipped the golden hooks into her earlobes, feeling the weight as the pearls swung at the sides of her jawline.

"Exquisite!" Daniella cried with delight. "I've never seen anyone wear them so perfectly."

Despite her misgivings, Lily smiled, loving Daniella's praise.

"It's happened," Daniella continued. "I saw it the moment you put on the earrings. You were meant to model."

Yes! That was exactly right. Lily's smile grew wider. She sat up straighter, pulling her shoulders back and lifting her chin. Every instruction she'd ever heard on *Model Mania* — to smile with your eyes, to let your inner beauty shine forth, to exude grace and poise — all made sense to her now. There was something about these earrings that freed her to be the sophisticated professional she'd always been meant to be.

"Perfect!" Daniella said, reaching for her brush. "You were destined for the Dolores Agonie collection. I'd even say you belong to it."

14

Hours later, Lily slumped with fatigue. But Daniella exuded vitality. Lily noticed the bright sparkle in the woman's blue eyes, and the pink in her cheeks. Daniella's hair even seemed to have more bounce to it.

"How are you doing there, Lily?" she asked, peeking around the side of her easel. "Feeling all right?"

Lily's stomach grumbled, demanding to be fed. Would it seem unprofessional to admit she was growing tired? It must nearly be time to leave. She had to call Amy.

"I'm okay," she fibbed.

Daniella came out from behind the easel. "Oh no, you're not okay," she observed, approaching Lily. "Your energy is flagging. How thoughtless of me to work you so hard!" As Daniella checked the small wristwatch she wore, she scowled. "We've been at it for three hours. When I get wrapped up in my work, the time simply flies."

Only three hours?! Lily felt as though she'd been there for days.

"I think you need to eat," Daniella said. "Come down from the stool and I'll find something for you."

Lily pulled the shawl more tightly around her shoulders.

"You're shivering, dear," Daniella noticed. "I'll turn the air-conditioning down as much as possible."

Sitting on the leather couch, Lily nodded. She really did feel hungry and cold, and a little dizzy, too. "Thanks."

Daniella looked into her half-size refrigerator and pulled out a container of yogurt. "Here!" She offered it to Lily along with a spoon. "This should revitalize you."

The doorbell rang, a melodic chiming sound. "Who could that be?" Daniella wondered. "I'm not expecting anyone. Excuse me. The bathroom is down the hall if you need it."

The yogurt did make Lily feel a bit better. At least her brain was less muddled. Standing, she glanced at the door. Daniella seemed to be arguing with someone, but Lily couldn't see the other person who stood in the hallway.

The cell phone in Lily's bag buzzed and Lily crossed to it. Maybe she could get cell service in here after all. Daniella might not realize it, but she'd said she didn't have a phone anyway.

"Hello?" Lily answered. She didn't hear anything, and pulled the phone away from her ear to check the number. But it wasn't her mother or Amy, and a shiver ran down Lily's spine. The call was from 000000! She tried again. "Hello?!" she repeated, hoping for more silence.

Then the whispering began, fast and impossible to understand. "Who is this?" Lily demanded. "This isn't funny."

The whispering got louder and wilder, as if other voices had joined the first. So many voices speaking at once! So impossible to understand what they were saying!

And the whispering seemed to be coming from

another source besides her phone. Holding the phone away, to her side, Lily listened closely.

The hallway! The whispering was also coming from the hallway.

Daniella was still over at the door speaking to someone on the other side as Lily walked toward the closed door in the hall. Gooseflesh formed on her arms. It was getting colder and colder.

Lily touched the door. It was freezing! Pressing her ear close, she heard a room filled with babbling voices — talking fast and all at once. They sounded agitated, and Lily strained to pick out just one of the voices she could understand, but it was impossible.

What did they want?

Were they real people? A TV? A recording?

Did she dare to turn the knob? Daniella hadn't told her she could go in there. But Lily just had to know. What was in there? Why was it calling her?

Lily listened again to her cell phone. The whispering call was still going.

Turning the knob, she cracked open the door. Icy air hit her face, instantly numbing her nose.

"What are you doing?" Daniella demanded before Lily could open the door fully.

Daniella sounded so angry that Lily opted for a lie. "Looking for the bathroom."

"Down the hall."

"Oh, sorry." Lily pulled the door shut and the voices stopped, both in the room and on her phone.

Lily hurried to the bathroom and stood inside, her heart pounding. She didn't know if she was more frightened of the voices or of Daniella. The woman was so furious with her one minute but then so sweet the next.

Her phone beeped to show her that she had almost no battery left on her phone, even though it had been fully charged when she left Amy's apartment. And there was definitely no cell service available, either. But then how had the whispering people called her?

Turning, Lily caught her own image in the mirror. Surprised at what she saw, Lily pulled back. Were her eyes playing tricks? She looked so much prettier than ever before. Had her cheekbones gotten higher? Her dark eyes seemed somehow deeper, more mysterious. How could this have happened?

But maybe Lily hadn't changed at all. Leaning in, she considered another idea. Could it be that being around the worldly, artistic Daniella had made her see her own true beauty for the first time?

Or was it the earrings?

The earrings glistened against her hair. What was it about them that made her feel so beautiful when she wore them? Sure, they were gorgeous, but it was more than that.

With the earrings on, Lily felt connected to all the beautiful girls in the portraits. They'd lived years ago, yet in the portraits they were captured at the height of their youth and beauty. It was as though they'd been frozen in time, never to change.

Shutting her eyes, Lily pictured the haggard old woman who had crawled out of the frame last night and she shivered at the memory. Was that what Julia had turned into so many years after her portrait had been painted — that horrifying, old, rotting woman?

Lily opened her eyes and gazed into the mirror.

She gasped sharply.

The ancient woman was back, staring at her from the other side of the mirror.

But it was different.

This woman wore a colorful shawl wrapped around her shoulders.

The old woman in the mirror was Lily!

Lᵢₗy ᵣₐcₑd into the hall and banged into
Daniella. She screamed, jumping back. "I want to
go!" Lily shouted as she hurried toward the front
door. "Let me go!"

"Oh, I've upset you Lily, dear. Please stop!"

Catching a glimpse of herself in the hall mirror, Lily paused. She wasn't old. She looked like
herself again.

But still . . . something very strange was going on.

Daniella came to her side. "I am so sorry I snapped at you before. It was only a reflex. I never let anyone into that room."

"But there are people in that room," Lily insisted, pointing at the door, her arm shaking with fear. "They were talking. I heard them. They called me on my phone! Who is in there?!"

Daniella smiled gently. "Don't be so worried, Lily. I'll show you what's in the room."

Lily's throat went dry and she coughed. Did she really want to know?

Taking hold of Lily's hand, Daniella drew Lily toward the room and opened the door. Lily stepped back, afraid of what she was about to see.

Inside was a desk and chair, with several storage cabinets on either side. Stepping in, Daniella took a key from the pocket of her white dress and unlocked the cabinet closest to the desk.

"This is who lives in this room," she said. The cabinet had four shelves, and on each shelf was a framed Dolores Agonie portrait, all upright and facing forward. "Here's where I store my priceless collection."

Lily followed Daniella into the room. She recognized the portraits of Rosalie, Ashlynne, Anne, and Emily. But the room was still extremely cold and Lily was sure she heard a low sound.

"And you have Julia, of course," Daniella said.

"Oh, of course," Lily said.

"The rest of them are in the other cabinets," Daniella said, gesturing around the room.

"The rest?"

"Yes, open any cabinet."

Lily approached a cabinet and pulled. Out slid

a stack of oil paintings on canvas — all portraits
of young women, each subject as lovely as the next.
Girls of every race and ethnicity — some plump-
cheeked, others lean and delicate, with every kind
of hair, nose, and mouth shape — smiled up at her.
Each exuded her own form of undeniable radi-
ance and charm.

Lily slid the cabinet closed and opened the one
above it. She gazed down at even more portraits.
These were the same as the others except that the
paintings appeared to be even older. The girls
wore ruff collars and high hats; others wore tribal
headdresses and elaborate feathers.

All of them were beautiful.

All of them wore the pearl earrings.

"They're all wonderful, aren't they?" Daniella
said. "The ones I displayed at the Haunted Museum
are my special prizes because of the superlative

quality of the painting, but I love them all so much. They're like a part of me. And soon you will be in this collection with them."

"And this might be the voices you heard," she continued. A rotary phone sat on the desk next to an old-fashioned answering machine. "Twelve messages, my, my," Daniella said. "And they all came in the last ten minutes." She pressed the PLAY button: *This is the Salvation Army, Ms. Artel. We wanted to thank you for your donation of used clothing. The women's outfits are so old-fashioned and sweet. I'm sure people will want them for costumes.*

Daniella, this is Jill. Don't forget we have a photo shoot this Saturday. Okay, babe, bye!

This is Yung's Dry Cleaning. Your order is ready to be picked up.

Lily felt increasingly foolish as she listened to Daniella's answering machine play. All the messages were from women, and all were spoken fast and low.

"But why would your machine call my cell phone?" Lily asked. "And why would they all be speaking at once?"

Daniella smiled and shrugged. "I'm the last person you should ask about why technology does the things it does. It's all mysterious to me."

It all sounded so logical, but Lily wasn't done.

"I looked in the bathroom mirror and I was old — really, really old. And ugly!" Lily cried, frustrated and frightened. "Why did that happen?"

Daniella tucked her hair behind her ear. "You've had a long day, Lily. You're exhausted and your imagination is overstimulated. I've seen it happen many times with new models."

"It's not that," Lily disagreed. "I'm feeling so chilly and tired. I don't know what it is."

"Perhaps you're coming down with something," Daniella suggested. She placed her smooth, cool hand on Lily's forehead. "I don't think you have a fever, yet you might be getting sick. No doubt that's why you looked odd in the mirror."

"No, I looked *old*," Lily insisted. She was getting tired of being told that the things she noticed weren't real. Why would she all of a sudden start seeing and hearing things? Amy and Daniella might want to find reasonable explanations for what was happening to her, but that didn't mean that they were right! "I was old. I saw it in the mirror," Lily repeated.

"Lily, dear, how could that be?" Daniella asked. Her tone made Lily feel as if she was being spoken to like she was a child and she resented it.

"I don't know," she admitted.

"Then does it make sense?" Daniella went on.

"No, I suppose it doesn't make sense," Lily replied.

"Perhaps you're not up to the strains of modeling," Daniella said, wandering away from Lily to gaze out the large window of her apartment. "Maybe it would be better to stop than to tire you out even more. You're overwrought. Not every girl has the strength and determination to make her dream come true."

"No! No! I'm up to it," Lily insisted. "Really! I am."

Daniella turned around and nodded, though her expression remained serious. "I hope you are, because you're quite beautiful. You really should be modeling."

"Thank you."

"I have to return some of those phone calls, so why don't you lie down or walk around a little;

whatever would make you feel better. We'll start again in fifteen minutes."

"All right," Lily said. "I'm sort of cold. I'm going to step outside the apartment to warm up."

"As you wish."

Lily started toward the apartment door, but Daniella leaped in front of her, blocking the way.

Lily stepped back, startled. "What's wrong?"

"You can't leave."

"Why not?"

Daniella held out her palm and stepped toward Lily. "The earrings. You can't take them out of the apartment."

Removing the earrings, Lily instantly felt lighter, and laughed at her mistake. "I forgot I had them on. Sorry."

16

Heat slammed into Lily the moment she stepped out of the apartment. The sudden change in temperature made her dizzy, and she put her hand on the wall to steady herself.

After a few slow breaths, Lily felt okay once more. She should call her mother and Aunt Amy. They'd want to know if she was all right.

But there was no sense in telling them she was

cold and exhausted and seeing images of her old age in the mirror. No reason to say that it was so frigid where she was that the moment she returned to the heat the change nearly knocked her to the floor.

They'd only worry. Plus, they might not allow her to return.

Lily decided it would be better to call at five when Amy was done with work and Lily was finished posing. Besides, she realized, patting her pocket, she'd left her phone in her bag back in the apartment.

Lily felt a wave of frozen air blow up the stairs and wondered what was causing it.

In the next moment, Julia stepped into view, stopping at the bottom landing of the stairs and looking up at Lily.

Lily gasped, and stepped back.

Julia was young once more in her gauzy dress.

Her black curls dangled into her face, and her large dark eyes stared seriously up at Lily.

Terrified, Lily backed up even more, flattening herself against Daniella's apartment door. "What do you want with me?" Lily asked, her voice a dry croak.

Julia lifted from the landing, effortlessly floating up until she hovered in the air over the stairs.

Lily turned her head away, not wanting to see, but when she glanced back again, Julia still hung there, gazing down at her with dark, sorrowful eyes. "What do you want?" Lily tried again.

Lily watched, both horrified and fascinated, as Julia's face became a mass of lines. They traveled down her arms, spreading along her outspread fingers. The sound of splitting flesh drew Lily's attention to Julia's ankles and feet where crisscross patterns emerged with lightning speed. Lily couldn't look away.

The hideous sight of Julia's erupting flesh reminded Lily of an old painted building that had been allowed to blister and peel in the sun. "No!" Lily cried as pieces of Julia's face flaked away, exposing the skeleton beneath.

"No!" she shouted again. Julia's hair was falling from her head, drifting down slowly like falling feathers. As patches fell away, the skin of her scalp was exposed, then it also began to flake away.

Soon Julia was a floating skeleton in a white dress. Only her eyes remained in the skull socket.

Whipping around, Lily pulled at the knob of Daniella's apartment but it wouldn't open. "Daniella!" she shouted, leaning on the doorbell. "Daniella!"

17

LILY?" AUDREEN stood at the bottom of the landing. "What's the matter?"

Couldn't Audreen see Julia? Lily pointed, and Julia's skull smiled ghoulishly at her, and she vanished.

Suddenly overwhelmed, Lily's knees gave out and she dropped to the floor, feeling completely drained.

Audreen climbed quickly to her side. "Are you all right? You look like you've . . . well you look ill."

"I'm so tired. And I don't know why Daniella isn't answering," Lily said. "I know she's there."

"Come to my place and rest," Audreen said. Lily allowed Audreen to draw her to standing and help her down the flight of stairs.

Audreen's apartment was cooled by a small air conditioner in the window. It was enough to take the brutal edge off the heat but didn't make the place feel like a freezer as Daniella's apartment did.

"I heard you shout when I stepped into the hall," Audreen explained as she poured some cold tap water into a glass for Lily. "What happened?"

"You didn't see anyone else on the stairs with me?" Lily asked.

"No . . . ," Audreen said. "But I felt a presence with us."

"There sure was," Lily told her. Lily didn't know if Audreen would believe her, or if she'd insist that Lily was imagining things like Aunt Amy and Daniella had. But she was so upset that she couldn't help telling her everything. "Daniella gave me one of her portraits and the girl in the painting is haunting me." She went on to tell Audreen about the sleepwalking and raining teeth and the video and the voices in the studio and how just now, the ghost had decayed right there in the air.

"It sounds to me like Julia's trying to tell you something about death and decay," Audreen said.

"But what?" Lily asked. A spirit with a message about death and decay wasn't exactly comforting.

"That's one of the first things we'll have to find out," Audreen replied thoughtfully.

Find out. Lily could have cried with relief. Someone wasn't telling her she was crazy, but thought she could figure out what was going on! Lily didn't feel quite as alone.

"Where's the portrait now?" Audreen asked.

"You're not going to believe this, but it disappeared this morning. Aunt Amy thought it reminded me of the Haunted Museum and gave me nightmares, so she wanted to give it back to Daniella. I'm sure we had it with us when we left this morning, but when we got here, it was just gone."

Audreen took the glass of water from Lily and set it on the table, then bent for something behind her couch. "Would this be it?" she asked, lifting the portrait.

Surprised, Lily stood. "Yes! That's it! How did you get it?"

"When I came home this morning from the coffeehouse where I eat breakfast it was leaning

against my door," Audreen said, setting the portrait down to lean against the side of the couch.

"I know Daniella just donated some of her portraits to the Haunted Museum and I wondered
if this could be one of them. I went to the exhibit
and thought I remembered this face. So I went
upstairs to ask Daniella if it belonged to her
because I thought it looked familiar. Didn't you
see me talking to her at her door?"

"That was you? I couldn't see who she was
speaking to."

"That was me. She's never been very neigh-
borly, but she seemed annoyed that I'd bothered
her and practically slammed the door in my face.
She said she knew where all her portraits were
and not to trouble her with nonsense again."

"That was rude," Lily remarked. "She has this
extremely cold room where she keeps lots and lots

of this kind of painting. Some of them were painted hundreds of years ago."

"That's probably why she has to keep them so cold," Audreen suggested, "to preserve them."

"Probably."

Audreen lifted the painting again and froze, studying it carefully. Slowly, she turned the portrait so that Lily could see it. The background colors were exactly as they'd always been.

But there was no one in the painting.

"It seems your girl has flown away," Audreen commented.

"See?!" Lily cried, sitting alongside Audreen. "This painting is haunted!"

"You don't have to convince me. I saw you surrounded by the dead, remember?"

"Where could she have gone?" Lily's voice rose fearfully, becoming squeaky with anxiety. "Why is this happening?"

"I don't know. Where did you first see this portrait?"

"The Haunted Museum. Daniella was there because she owns the portraits. She noticed how much I liked that painting in particular, so she gave it to me."

"Was there anything special about the painting? Or did anyone follow you out of the museum? Why would Daniella have given it to you?"

"I noticed all the paintings in the collection had the same earrings, but that's it. Why? Do you think all this has something to do with the museum, or with the paintings?"

"It might be, either. But I know a lot of other spiritualists and mediums here in the city. We talk. I hear things about that Haunted Museum."

"What kinds of things?" Lily asked.

"It's a lot older than people realize — and a lot spookier, too. There are stories about objects vanishing from their displays and turning up else-where, sometimes years later. There are stories of items kind of following people home, things from the museum that they shouldn't have touched."

Lily remembered the chill she'd felt when she'd studied the portraits. Had she touched one of them? "Do you mean this could all be my fault?"

"It doesn't matter whose fault it is, does it?" Audreen said. "It's more important to find out what's going on. We need more information."

"Are you going to contact the spirit world?" Lily asked hopefully.

"Not yet," Audreen replied. "I'm going to start with the Internet. And you'd better get back to Daniella."

18

LILY ROSE from the couch, but she didn't want to leave. She glanced at the painting that was now an empty background in a frame. She didn't even want to go out into the hallway. What if Julia was out there?

What if Lily just never went back?

But there was the modeling contract to think of.

"Come back here when you're done and I'll let you know if I find out anything," Audreen said.

Lily took a deep breath and exhaled slowly to calm herself. What was she so worried about?

Daniella might snap once in a while, but she was basically thoughtful and nice. And the fashion shoot she offered was an awesome chance. Lily knew it could take her years to be seen in an ad otherwise. Her future as a model might not happen at all without this. "All right," Lily said as she headed for the door. "I'll be back soon."

Audreen was already absorbed in the glow of the screen as she sat with her laptop balanced on her lap. She didn't seem to hear Lily.

Lily turned back to repeat her good-bye, but out of the corner of her eye she saw a young female figure glide out of Audreen's kitchen and into her bedroom.

Lily froze in place, her hand still on the knob.

"Audreen," she said in a choked whisper. "Someone is in your apartment."

Looking up from her laptop, Audreen scowled. "Is it Julia?"

Lily shook her head. This figure had blond hair piled high on her head and wore a blue embroidered gown. "It's another girl from one of the portraits, though." Lily recalled the girl called Ashlynne from the 1600s.

Getting up slowly, Audreen joined Lily by the door. "Maybe you should go," she suggested.

"I'm not going to leave you here alone with . . . her," Lily said.

Nodding, Audreen quietly pulled open a drawer of her nearby desk and picked out a tied bundle of some kind of herb. "Sage," she whispered. Taking out a box of matches from the same drawer, she lit the sage. Rather than burst into flame, the sage burned slowly, giving off lots of smoke and a pleasant aroma. "For some reason the dead don't like this smoke. It's a good way to clear a place of unwanted spirits."

Audreen ventured forward with the sage held in front of her. Her heart beating fast, Lily followed. She was close behind when Audreen entered the bedroom.

They saw the ghostly figure immediately.

She'd taken some daisies from a vase next to Audreen's bed and was scattering them into the air, singing a sad song that sounded very old. "My love doth weep for I do sleep, evermore in the cold, hard ground." She danced with her back to Audreen and Lily, tossing the daisy petals.

"It doesn't look like she's in the cold, hard ground to me," Audreen whispered with grim humor as she held the bundle of sage behind her back.

The sound of Audreen's voice startled the spirit, who whirled around to face them.

"You're pretty," Ashlynne said to Lily, her voice a high singsong. "I was pretty, once."

"You're still pretty," Lily found the nerve to say. There was something so sorrowful about the spirit girl that Lily wanted to make her feel better.

"Why are you here?" Audreen asked.

When the spirit girl spoke again, her voice became a low growl. "Because *she* touched us!" The spirit girl pointed at Lily. "Her touch awoke Julia, and Julia woke up the rest of us."

"The rest?" Audreen asked.

"The girls with the pearls. We can't go to the other side because part of us still lives here on this earthly plane. In order to go through, we need all our life force, and she took it."

"Who took it?" Lily asked.

"Dolores Agonie!" Ashlynne shouted, shaking her fist furiously. "Dolores Agonie! Curse her!"

"How did she do it?" Audreen asked. "How did Dolores Agonie trap your spirits?"

Ashlynne stopped and sniffed the air. Her face collapsed in an expression of disgust. "That smell! I have to leave."

Audreen tossed the bundle of sage behind her into the kitchen sink, but it was too late.

"Nooooooooo!" Ashlynne shrieked as her once lovely form began changing into a charred wreck. Gray ash flew from her as it engulfed her from the feet up.

Lily turned away in horror but still smelled the smoldering cinders as they piled up on the floor. Audreen stepped toward the ashes but they formed themselves into a column, rising into the air and escaping through the open window. Audreen and Lily watched the gray pillar swirling up into the sky until it disappeared.

"The girls with the pearls?" Audreen repeated. "Does that make any sense to you?"

Shaken by what she'd just seen, Lily slumped onto the bed, nodding her head.

"What? What does it mean?" Audreen prodded.

"The earrings," Lily said. "Remember, I noticed they all had the same earrings? But what does it mean?"

"I don't know, but it's time to do a reading and see what I can find out."

19

LILY AND Audreen sat side by side on the couch as Audreen dealt out strange-looking cards facedown onto the low coffee table. "These might look like tarot cards," Audreen said, "but they're not. This deck is modeled on the one they found in King Tut's tomb. It's much more ancient than tarot, but the idea is the same."

When her cards were dealt, Audreen turned the first card and let out a low whistle.

"What?" Lily asked.

"This is the death card."

Lily saw a skull with worms crawling out the eye sockets. The next card was a woman who wore a tall Egyptian hat, her eyes rimmed in kohl. "Nefertiti card," Audreen told Lily. "The positive side of this card is beauty, but the negative side is excessive vanity."

Death and vanity. Somehow it seemed they were on the right track. Just then there was a loud knock on the door.

Audreen opened the door and Amy entered. Immediately, her aunt rushed to sit beside Lily on the couch. "You're so pale! Are you sick?" Amy asked, distressed.

Audreen and Lily told Amy what they'd just experienced and about Julia having escaped from the painting. "I guess when Lily touched that painting of Julia, she stirred up some unhappy spirits," Audreen said.

"Don't fill her head with all your craziness," Amy insisted. "Next you'll be charging us a hundred dollars an hour to get rid of the evil spirits."

"I'm not charging anyone anything," Audreen defended herself.

"She's helping me with this haunting," Lily said.

"And what's all this?" Amy asked, sweeping her hands above the cards on the coffee table.

"I'm just trying to figure out what's happening," Audreen replied. "Lily's in real danger."

"Believing a faker like you is the only danger she's in," Amy shot back.

"Aunt Amy, stop," Lily said. "We're not making this up. Look at the painting now!"

Audreen handed the painting to Amy. Lily was relieved that Julia remained missing from the painting.

Still looking doubtful, Amy examined the painting, turning it front and back. Lily hoped this would be enough to change her aunt's mind. What could Amy say after seeing this proof? She had to be convinced now.

"I'm sorry, but you could have rigged this up," Amy said, giving the painting back to Audreen. "It doesn't prove anything."

"I'd have to be a fast worker to paint that this morning with enough time for it to dry," Audreen said. "Plus, I didn't know anything about any of this until just now."

Lily glanced at Audreen's alarm clock. "Aunt Amy, why are you here?" she asked. "It's not even two o'clock yet."

"Daniella phoned me," Amy explained. "She said you took a break and never came back, and wondered if I knew where you'd gone. I was frantic, Lily. I rushed right over here. What were you thinking?"

"I'm sorry, Aunt Amy, but I saw a ghost on the

stairway and then Audreen came when she heard me screaming. I was about to go back to Daniella's when the second ghost showed up."

"I'm sure you were," Amy said, rolling her eyes skeptically. "And what are you burning in here? Incense?"

Suddenly reminded, Audreen hurried into the kitchen and picked up the smoldering sage, stubbing out the last cinders in the sink. Untying it, she separated out a bunch and wrapped a rubber band around it. "Keep this with you, just in case," she said, handing the sage to Lily.

"Oh, please," Amy moaned. "Give me a break." She turned to Lily. "Come on. I have to tell Daniella that I've found you. She's so worried."

"Good-bye, Audreen. Thank you," Lily said.

"Call if you need me," Audreen replied, handing Lily her card.

"Lily won't need that," Amy said impatiently, but Lily pocketed the card anyway.

"Don't forget your painting," Audreen said, offering the empty painting.

"You keep it," Amy said as she and Lily left the apartment.

20

OUTSIDE IN the hall, Amy stopped and turned to Lily. "I'm sorry if you think I was rude. But I've been so worried! If I hadn't thought to look for you in that apartment I'd be out searching all over the city. Plus, I don't trust her. The city is full of these so-called mystics who are all frauds." Amy put her hand on her forehead and breathed deeply, trying to calm herself.

"Maybe they're not all phonies," Lily said. "It could be that only some of them are. I trust Audreen. Besides, why didn't you just call me?"

"I did call you! I called like a hundred times!"

Lily had forgotten that her bag was still up in Daniella's apartment. "Sorry, Aunt Amy. I didn't want to worry you. I couldn't call you from Daniella's because she has no cell service at her place. She's got no computer, no Wi-Fi at all. I left my phone there when I went to get some fresh air."

"Do you feel well enough to finishing the posing with her?" Amy asked as they headed up the stairs back to Daniella's apartment.

"I was feeling sort of weird before, but now I'm okay."

When they rang Daniella's doorbell, she answered immediately. "Thank heavens you're safe!" she cried as she let Amy and Lily in.

The moment she was inside, Lily hugged herself for warmth. She'd almost forgotten that Daniella's apartment was like a freezer. Amy rubbed her own arms for warmth also.

"Sorry I worried you," Lily apologized. How honest did she want to be with Daniella? Lily wasn't certain. If she told the whole story, would Daniella be frightened off from working with Lily? Despite everything, Lily didn't want to lose her shot at the modeling contract.

"Lily felt sick and the woman downstairs helped her out," Amy told Daniella.

"Do you mean that so-called psychic?" Daniella asked disdainfully.

"Audreen," Lily put in.

"Stay away from her," Daniella advised. "That young woman is a complete charlatan."

"A what?" Lily asked.

"A fake! A phony! A crook!"

"She's not a crook," Lily objected. "She never asked me for any money."

"Well, you watch yourself with her," Daniella warned. "Lily, I have to tell you that I don't feel that our first session went well — not at all."

"I'm sorry, Daniella," Lily replied, flushing.

"She was probably just nervous," Amy added. "She's been so excited and wants to be perfect right away."

"I don't know," Daniella said. "My time is very valuable. I can't afford another lost day like today."

"But it wasn't a total loss," Lily insisted. She couldn't lose this chance almost before it had even begun. "You painted all morning. Can I see what you did?"

"I'd love to see it, too," Amy added enthusiastically.

Daniella led them around to see the canvas she'd been painting on. Although most of it remained unfinished, the background and the outlines of Lily's face were painted. The background was the same swirl of color that the other portraits had. "It's going to look just like the other Dolores Agonie paintings," Amy said. "Where did you learn to paint this way, Daniella?"

"I learned from my grandmother who was also a member of the Agonie clan. It's a style passed down among the women in our family. We're all descendants of Lucrezia Borgia, you know."

"Oh really," Amy said with a scowl.

Daniella smiled. "Oh, I know Lucrezia has some bad press. People say she was a poisoner and all sorts of evil things, but history has distorted the true stories. She was a remarkable woman, actually."

Amy and Daniella continued to discuss Lucrezia Borgia, but Lily wasn't paying attention. She'd begun by casually looking at the swirling background behind her portrait, but now she couldn't stop staring at it.

It was as though the colors had somehow hypnotized her. They moved on their own, creating a tunnel of color that pulled Lily into it. She felt as though she were rising out of her body and heading into the swirling vortex of color.

21

LILY!"

Lily's eyes opened and she was in Amy's arms, both of them on the floor of Daniella's apartment. "You fainted," Amy said as Lily leaned forward, still lightheaded. "Are you okay?"

Lily nodded shakily.

"It's been a long day," Daniella said, helping Lily to her feet as Amy stood. "Have some lemonade and cheese, then we'll start again tomorrow."

"Thank you." Lily felt so foolish. She'd never fainted before. From the corner of her eye she saw the swirling colors of the unfinished portrait but looked away quickly, not wanting to be caught up again in its strange power.

Amy and Lily said good-bye to Daniella and rode the subway home. The train was less crowded than it had been in the rush-hour morning since it was now the middle of the day, and so they were able to sit.

"What do you think of Daniella?" Lily asked Amy.

"She's sort of old-fashioned," Amy said. "You know, the way her makeup and hair and clothing are so perfect. A little vain, too, and very preoccupied with energy and spirits for an artist with a fashion background. But her paintings are lovely, and those sculptures in her apartment . . ."

"Do you like her?" Lily asked.

Amy hesitated. "I'm not sure. She's certainly an impressive artist. We don't know her that well."

"You judged Audreen pretty quickly and we'd only just met her," Lily reminded her.

"At least Daniella's not filling your head with spooky ghosts and burning sage."

Lily opened her mouth to tell Amy that it wasn't Audreen's fault. Something strange really was going on. But she decided not to say anything more about it. It was pretty obvious by now that Amy didn't believe in the spirit world or anything mystical.

Lily was frightened though — really frightened. Who knew when a ghost would appear again?

They left the subway and stopped for pizza at a shop on the way to Amy's apartment. Just before they got to Amy's front door, they bought ice-cream cones from a truck. "Don't worry, Lily,"

Amy said, licking her cone. "Everything will be okay."

"I hope so," Lily replied, still thinking of Daniella and Julia and the new ghost from that afternoon.

Back in Amy's building, they took the elevator up and walked down the hall. "I don't believe it," Amy muttered.

A package wrapped in brown paper was leaning against the front door. From its size and shape it wasn't hard to guess the contents. Someone had left a portrait at the front door.

• • •

Inside the apartment, Lily sat on a chair and tore at the paper. "Audreen probably returned Julia's frame," she said.

But as the wrapping fell away, Lily and Amy stared down, surprised. It was a portrait of the girl from the 1800s, the one named Emily. She wore a serious expression, though her green eyes were lively with interest. Brown ringlets framed her pale, heart-shaped face, and a lace collar ringed her neck. Her mouth bowed sweetly.

"Daniella probably felt bad about today and sent this painting as a gift," Amy said.

"But why would she do that?" Lily asked. "These paintings are so special to her. Why would she give another one to me?"

"I don't know," Amy admitted. "She is a bit eccentric. We'll ask her tomorrow."

That night Amy and Lily sat and thumbed through some fashion magazines Amy had brought from work. "You could totally succeed in modeling," Amy said. "You're even prettier than a lot of these girls."

From time to time, Lily glanced at the portrait of Emily, which she'd propped up on the dresser in the same spot where Julia's picture had once been. Part of her was afraid that Emily would climb out of her portrait just as Julia had, but she tried to shake the feeling off. It was just a pretty painting of a pretty girl. There was no reason to be afraid of it.

The weather was still steamy, though the fans by the open window gave them some relief. "You don't have to tie us together tonight," Lily said when she saw Amy yawn and stretch. "I'll be all right."

Amy's expression was doubtful. "Are you sure?"

"Positive." Truly Lily wasn't so sure but she wanted to believe everything would be fine tonight. She wanted the nightmares to stop, and to finally get a good night's sleep.

Amy slid off the bed and headed for the kitchen. "I have an idea," she said. In three minutes she returned, her arms full with cans, glasses, vases, and even a bell.

"What's all that for?" Lily asked.

Amy began lining the things on the floor about a foot in front of the window. "You won't be able to sleepwalk near the window without knocking over all this stuff. I'll keep my door open so I'll be sure to hear it."

When she finished, Amy went to the front door and bolted every latch. "I don't normally lock every single one of these but I'm not taking any chances tonight." She headed toward her bedroom but hesitated. "I really don't mind sleeping on the pull-out."

"I'll be fine!" Lily said. "Really!"

"All right, then. Good night."

" 'Night."

Amy switched off the light, and Lily stretched out on the bed. Just as the night before, the white lace curtains fluttered in the fan's breeze. They reminded Lily of how Julia had appeared and lured her to the window. With a nervous shiver, Lily turned over to face away from them.

As tense as she was, especially with Emily looking on, Lily was exhausted and soon drifted off to sleep. She dreamed that she was home and playing soccer with some of her best friends. She was happy and laughing as she scored a goal.

But her eyes snapped open suddenly. Her skin tingled with freezing goose bumps. Something icy was pressing hard against her back.

22

LILY WAS too terrified to do anything but lie there, shivering in the dark. Beside her, whatever was there began to sob.

Slowly Lily turned to face it.

"Aunt Amy!" Lily tried to shout but her voice was a squeak of fear. The bloated, bluish girl beside her could have been Emily — if she had been floating under water for many years. What were once brown curls now stood out from her head like tangled seaweed. Her skin and lips were swollen, and her dark-rimmed eyes bulged. And her dress was shredded and tinged green and brown.

Despite her repulsive appearance, Emily's sobs were so heart-wrenching that Lily couldn't help but feel sympathy for her. "What's wrong?" she asked.

"Dolores Agonie," Emily sobbed. "Dolores Agonie."

"I don't understand."

"I can't die but I'm dead!" Emily shouted. "They buried me at sea but I can't rest!"

"Lily?" Amy called sleepily from her bedroom.

"Why can't you die?" Lily asked, ignoring her aunt for the moment.

"Part of my spirit is trapped in this world. I can't cross over without that part."

"Lily?" Amy appeared in the bedroom doorway, rubbing her eyes. "What's going on?"

Before Lily could reply, Emily broke into an anguished howl so deafening Lily had to cover her ears. Amy stood there, also shielding her ears with clenched fists, cringing.

Tears gushed from Emily's swollen eyes, spilling waves of water into the room. As she cried, Emily floated toward the ceiling, her arms and legs spread wide as though she were drifting under the ocean. The torrent of salty tears spilling from her eyes was quickly filling the room with water.

Still holding her hands over her ears, Lily sloshed through the knee-high water to Amy's side. Together they clawed at the front door, frantically trying to undo the locks as the water rose around them.

They were waist deep in water when the last lock was opened but the door wouldn't budge. Lily glanced at the open window and saw water pouring out, but still it continued to rise.

"Emily, stop!" Lily shouted but her voice was drowned in the overwhelming roar of the girl's howl. The blast from Emily's mouth worked like a wind over the water, stirring it up into waves and whirlpools.

One hand still covering her ear, Amy pointed to the dresser and Lily understood that it was something they could stand on as the water continued to climb. When they were on top of it, the water was once more down around their knees.

Things in the apartment started to float, pitched to and fro on the choppy water. As Emily's portrait bobbed by, Lily wasn't surprised to see that the girl's image was no longer in it.

The whirring fan sparked as the water hit it, and then spun to a stop. Pictures lifted from their hooks and floated off the walls. Books, magazines, pencils, and any odd item that was light enough to float became unmoored and drifted in the ocean of tears. Heavy items toppled and then sunk.

Lily flailed, splashing as the water rose to her chin. It wouldn't be long before she and Amy were completely underwater. Cracks were forming in the walls, splitting under the pressure from Emily's tears.

In the next minutes the water rose to the ceiling. Lily clutched Amy's arm as they floated there. Emily dangled just below them, her howl silenced by the water.

Lily gripped Amy tighter as they swam, desperately trying to keep their noses in the inches of air still left at the ceiling. They were going to drown!

"I'm sorry! I'm sorry!" Emily cried. "I wanted to tell you something important — but I'm so sad. This always happens when I cry."

"Just try to stop crying!" Lily said to her.

"I can't! It's going to happen to you, too. It's so sad!"

And then suddenly, it all disappeared. Emily and the water caused by her tears vanished.

In the next second, Lily and Amy crashed to the floor.

. . .

Lily and Amy sat on the pull-out bed in stunned silence for fifteen minutes. Lily's right knee and elbow throbbed from the impact of the fall. Amy had hit the back of her head and kept rubbing at it.

There could be no doubt that what they'd just experienced had been real — they'd both lived it. But nothing was wet. All Amy's things that had been strewn across the apartment, shaken loose and soaked — they were all now dry and back to normal.

Amy never would have believed her. But this time she'd seen it for herself.

Finally Lily spoke. "Do you believe me now?"

"Uh-huh," Amy answered, still sounding shocked. "I definitely do. I don't think we should have anything more to do with these portraits. Or with Daniella Artel."

Lily nodded in agreement, but she wasn't sure that getting away from the spirits was going to be so easy. "But what if they keep showing up at the apartment?"

23

W<small>HEN</small> I get to work I'll call Daniella to tell her you're not coming," Amy said as she pulled on her sandals the next morning. "Would you mind very much just staying in today?"

Lily still rested on the pull-out couch, feeling bruised and off-balance from yesterday. "I don't mind, but what are you going to tell Daniella?"

"I'll tell her a sort of truth — that you're too

weirded out by the idea of being a Dolores Agonie portrait. You don't want to wind up with your face in the Haunted Museum."

"Okay." Lily glanced at the blank portrait, now lying on the floor. Though many of Amy's things had been rearranged by the flood, the painting's background seemed fine. The image of Emily, however, had not returned to it.

"Okay, I'm going," Amy announced, though she hesitated by the door. "Don't leave the apartment, okay?"

"Okay," Lily agreed.

Lily sat in the quiet apartment. She was scared now that Amy had left. Would one of the ghosts come back, or would they stay away now that she wasn't sitting for the Dolores Agonie portrait? What if a new one appeared while she was there alone? What did they want?

Suddenly there was a loud knock on the door. Lily's heart jumped a beat. What if it was another painting being delivered?

Lily peered into the door's security peephole. Audreen stood on the other side, waiting.

"How did you find me?" Lily asked as she opened the door.

"Daniella has your address," Audreen informed her, walking in. "I went up to ask for it and she gave it to me. Is she ever upset with *you*!"

"Really?" Lily cringed a little. In spite of everything that had happened, she felt bad about letting Daniella down.

"Why didn't you go back?" Audreen asked, gazing around the apartment.

"Wait until you hear this," Lily began and then launched into her tale of the previous night's events.

Audreen became more and more wide-eyed

with astonishment as Lily spoke. "Then why isn't everything damp now?" she asked when Lily had finished her story.

"Emily's ghost cried and cried until the water reached the ceiling. It was like the ocean in here. And then suddenly it was all back to normal. Amy experienced it, too, so I didn't imagine it."

"I guess it's true then," Audreen said.

"What's true?" Lily asked.

Audreen propped herself on the end of the pull-out bed. "I did some searching online about the Dolores Agonie portraits and uncovered some bizarre stuff."

"What?" Lily asked, righting an overturned straight-back chair so she could sit on it.

Audreen pulled a folded printout from the pocket of her shorts. "Listen to this," she said and began to read: CURSED PORTRAITS A HIT AT HAUNTED MUSEUM.

There's something the downtown Haunted Museum is not telling you. In their display titled Sinister Portraits, the collection painted by generations of artists all named Dolores Agonie is perhaps the most frightening. Though the girls portrayed span centuries, they have more in common than just the luminous pearl earrings they wear and the name of the artist who captured their beauty, youth, and vitality. Every subject was dead by the age of thirteen.

Lily's hands flew to her cheeks. "Could that be true? How could they know that about Ashlynne and Rosalie?" Lily asked. "There were no newspapers around in their time, were there?"

"Family stories passed down through the generations," Audreen replied.

"Are there any pictures of Dolores Agonie?" Lily asked.

"Sort of — but you can't ever tell what she looks like. She's always under a big hat or turned away or wearing sunglasses and a scarf. You can see a family resemblance to Daniella, though. The women are obviously related."

Audreen spread the pictures she'd printed out on the bed. One of them was a very old engraving of Dolores Agonie's face, but ink had been smeared across it, covering the details. Lily could see what Audreen meant about the resemblance, though. All the women were graceful and probably had been attractive.

"So is it her, or the girls in the paintings haunting me?" Lily asked. "What do the spirits want from me?"

"To warn you of something," Audreen guessed. "Or to frighten you off. They might need your help, or they might be jealous because you're alive and they aren't. I don't know exactly, and we didn't get to finish that reading yesterday."

"So it sounds like there's nothing I can do to make it stop," Lily said. "I'm glad you came by, Audreen. I'm scared being here all alone."

"I can't stay," Audreen said. "I teach a class in palm reading this afternoon, and I have clients who come to my apartment, too. I have to go back."

"Could I hang out at your place?" Lily asked. "That way if something did happen at least I won't be alone."

"Okay," Audreen agreed. "Let's get some breakfast and text Amy so she knows where you are. You don't want to scare her a second time. Will she mind if you come to my place?"

"I'm sure she won't. After last night, she's convinced that this is for real."

"All right, then. Let's go."

24

AUDREEN'S FIRST client was waiting at Audreen's front door when she and Lily arrived. Audreen was teaching her to read tarot cards, and Lily was glad she was there. The more people the better.

Audreen offered Lily headphones so she could curl up in a big easy chair to watch TV without bothering the tarot card lesson. Reruns of *Model Mania*'s last season were playing, which was just what Lily needed. She loved how the viewers got to know each girl and learn why winning a modeling contract was so important to her. By the first commercial break, she was wishing she could compete for the contract.

In this episode, the models went to Paris to meet top fashion designers. The young women looked so gorgeous in the latest collections, and Lily wondered if she'd thrown away her one chance to be a model. Was being frightened a good reason to give up on her dream? After all, once the portrait was done, Daniella would use her in the fashion photo shoot and all the Dolores Agonie stuff would be over with. It might have only been another day of posing for the portrait and it would all be over. She'd been so stupid!

Lily was on her third episode of *Model Mania* when she started to feel tired again. She had to be getting sick.

Audreen was consulting with a man who

wanted to make contact with his mother who had recently died. Lily glanced at her before taking off the headphones and resting her head on the arm of the chair. In minutes, she drifted off to sleep.

When Lily awoke again sometime later, the apartment doorbell was ringing. A note on the coffee table said:

Have gone to teach my lesson.
Back in two hours. Audreen.

Had Audreen forgotten her keys? Lily chained the top lock before unlocking the rest of the door. "Who's there?" she asked.

Someone spoke, but the voice was too low for Lily to make out, so she opened the door just a crack.

"Lily!" Daniella cried in surprise. "What are you doing here?" Lily thought the woman looked younger and more beautiful than she had the day before. Why had she thought the woman was in her forties? Daniella had to be in her early thirties.

Embarrassed that she'd stood Daniella up, Lily opened the door fully, feeling completely awkward. "Hello, Daniella. I hope you're not angry at me. I wasn't feeling well. Aunt Amy called you, didn't she?"

Daniella didn't seem annoyed as she stepped into Audreen's apartment. "I completely understand. In fact, I came by to ask Audreen if she'd seen you, since she came by this morning to get Amy's address. I wanted to know how you were. Why are you here?"

"I didn't like being alone, so Audreen said I could stay with her."

"That was foolish. You could have come to stay with me."

"I didn't want to bother you."

"It wouldn't be a bother. How are you feeling now?"

"Not very good," Lily said honestly. Despite just having woken from a nap, she was still tired and her head had started to throb.

"It's this beastly heat. It just pulls the energy right out of you. Audreen's air-conditioning is hardly doing the job."

Lily realized that she did feel unusually warm even though the air conditioner was blowing.

"I have an idea!" Daniella said. "You'll come to my place and finish sitting for the portrait! It's so much cooler. Sit on the couch instead of on the stool, and once I paint in your beautiful eyes, you can sleep while I finish your portrait."

"Do you think you can finish today?" Lily asked.

"Of course."

"And — are you still considering me for the fashion photo shoot?" Lily dared to ask, encouraged by Daniella's pleasant manner.

"Oh, absolutely! I'm sure you'd be perfect for it," Daniella said. "You have to build up some stamina for the long days but I'm confident that you're the right girl for the job. With a gorgeous model like you, the line will sell itself!"

Even though Lily felt tired, a smile crossed her face. The chance to be a model wasn't gone, after all. "Oh, thank you, Daniella! Thank you!" she said, thrilled.

Daniella stepped back out into the hall, beckoning Lily to follow. "Come on, Lily, let's just get this done."

"I need to leave Audreen a note."

"Oh, don't bother," Daniella said. "You'll be back before she even returns."

"All right," Lily agreed, joining Daniella in the hall. She followed her up the stairs into her cold apartment.

DANIELLA TOOK the pearl earrings from the locked drawer and presented them to Lily.

"They're so much bigger than they were yesterday!" Lily said, surprised.

"Do you think so?" Daniella asked lightly, examining the earrings in her hand. "They seem the same to me."

"No. They're larger," Lily insisted.

Daniella placed the earrings in Lily's hand. "They don't feel heavier, do they?"

Lily had to admit that they didn't. They reminded her of a balloon that had been pumped with more air. Besides, she didn't want to argue with Daniella, not when she'd been given this second chance. "I guess I just didn't remember them right," Lily said.

"Of course. That's it," Daniella said. "Put them on now and let's get to work."

Lily slipped the earrings on while Daniella once more draped the colorful scarf around her. She sat on the couch as Daniella moved her easel over.

Daniella started painting, murmuring praise as she went. "Such gorgeous eyes — so young and bright. How I envy you!"

As she sat there posing, Lily felt herself tiring again. Her back ached, and her head felt fuzzy from exhaustion. Even though Daniella's place was like an ice box, Lily felt hot. Maybe it was some kind of flu — but in the summer?

"Almost done with the eyes," Daniella said sweetly. "Then you can sleep through the rest of it."

"That would be good," Lily croaked, her mouth dry.

After a while more, Daniella smiled. "All right, Lily. You can sleep now."

Lily's eyes slid shut, and she was asleep in moments. She dreamed she was in a desert and the sun was drying her up, and then she dreamed that her teeth were coming lose and that she couldn't see. When she awoke, she had no idea how long she'd been asleep, but she felt terrible, and knew something was very wrong.

Lily attempted to get off the couch but stumbled when her legs couldn't support her.

Her legs! They had turned into two sticks, laced with deeply purple veins. She checked her hands and gasped. They were gnarled, with knobs at each joint and thick, yellowed fingernails.

Where was Daniella?

Lily leaned on the furniture as she pulled herself toward the bathroom. Once there, she threw her weight heavily on the sink for support as she peered into the mirror.

Lily was beyond old — ancient! Dark, ringed eyes gazed back at her from the mirror, sunken into a face etched with deep, deep wrinkles. She'd lost nearly all her hair — and what she still had was a wiry white.

Daniella appeared in the bathroom doorway. Lily saw her reflected in the mirror and turned.

Daniella's blond hair now swung buoyantly at her shoulders. Her skin glowed, and she had the fit, athletic figure of a teenage girl. Beneath her smirking smile, she sucked on a hard candy.

"What have you done to me?" Lily meant to shout but it came out as a cracked whisper.

Daniella's eyes were bright with merriment as she spit into her hand the candy she'd been sucking on.

The pearls!

And the pearls had changed again. They'd grown very small, like tiny, shriveled white raisins.

"Yes, you guessed it," Daniella said smugly. "I've sucked the life right out of you."

"I don't understand," Lily said, clutching the towel rack to support herself.

"Remember that story about the pearls being a gift from a demon?"

Lily remembered.

"And remember I told you how much I liked that story?"

Lily recalled that, too, and nodded.

"Well, I like it because it's true. That's how I've stayed young and beautiful for centuries. The pearls absorb your youth, and when I suck on the pearls . . ." She twirled to display her new young beautiful self. "You see the results. It's so effective I only have to renew it about once a century."

Lily felt so weak she had to sit on the edge of the bathtub. Her head was so heavy she could hardly lift it. "What now?" she asked. "I need to get back."

"Oh no, dear. You're so weak, like a little bird. I have a plane to catch, but before I go, I think I should take you up to the roof. Maybe we can make you fly away before I leave."

"No," Lily whimpered as Daniella tugged at her arms. "I won't go to the roof."

"I'm afraid you don't have too much choice, granny," Daniella said with a chuckle.

Lily tried to struggle with Daniella, but nothing she did made a difference. She was just too weak.

26

Up on the roof, Lily felt even worse. It was yet another humid, blazing hot day and she could hardly catch her breath in the muggy air.

Daniella dragged her to the edge of the roof where a three-foot wall ran along the side. "You gave me such a difficult time, Lily. And I was getting weak, which was even worse. If I don't recharge, I get old very quickly. My time was running out."

"The spirits are draining you," Lily whispered. "They're coming to get back at you."

"Oh, them! They act up anytime they sense me getting weak. One or two of them pops out of a painting and tries to get me, and for nothing every time. I let you have Julia because you touched her in the museum. That energized her, and I knew she would go to you anyway. The rest of them are safely locked away, though."

Lily realized that Daniella was mistaken. Ashlynne and Emily were also loose. Julia had freed them. Maybe Rosalie and Anne had also been freed — at least Lily hoped so.

"They're trapped," Lily croaked. "They have to stay on earth because you hold part of them captive. They'll never leave you alone."

"Did Julia tell you that?" Daniella asked. "Have you been *talking* to her?" She tossed her head back and rocked with laughter.

"It's been nice chatting with you, granny, but it's time for you to go bye-bye," Daniella said. She hauled Lily up onto the ledge. Glancing down, Lily saw that it was a straight drop to the corner parking lot below. Panicked and terrified, Lily gripped Daniella's wrist with her last bit of strength.

Daniella shook her hard, trying to break loose. It took all Lily's willpower to hang on . . . and she didn't think she could do it much longer. Kicking with the last of her strength, Lily managed to push the two of them back from the wall a few feet.

"Give up, brat," Daniella snarled. "I'm stronger than you'll ever be again."

Lily continued to struggle, bending and twisting her torso so Daniella couldn't get a hold of her.

As Lily struggled, the air around them lost its brutal heat. Lily realized gooseflesh had risen on her arms. And that sound — the one she'd thought was air-conditioning that day in Daniella's locked room — it was back.

And out of the corner of her eye, Lily noticed a circle of feet surrounding them — bent, twisted, ancient feet.

Five haggard old women surrounded them: Julia, Emily, Ashlynne, Rosalie, and Anne.

And there were more figures, dimly visible, hovering above the five she could see clearly. They were the other girls whose portraits she'd seen in the cabinets.

Lily suddenly knew that the sound she heard that day wasn't air-conditioning. It was the thrum of hundreds of heartbeats!

Daniella's apartment wasn't super air-conditioned at all! It was filled with the spirits of the dead!

"Give us back what you have stolen!" Julia demanded of Daniella.

Daniella looked up, stunned, and her expression changed from rage to shock to terror. "Leave me alone, you old women."

"You're the old woman!" Rosalie shrieked. "Hundreds of years old! You sucked out our youth and then you killed us."

"You smothered me in a hole covered with dirt," Julia said.

"You trapped me in a burning building," Ashlynne said.

"You drowned me in the ocean," said Emily.

"You shot me," Anne said.

"You stabbed me," said Rosalie.

"If I killed you, then why aren't you *dead*?" Daniella asked, backing away from them.

"We can't die while we live inside of you," Julia said.

Lily broke free from Daniella's grip.

"Lucrezia Borgia, you stole our youth, our beauty, and our souls," Rosalie said. "We will never retrieve our lives but we want our souls."

Daniella laughed haughtily at them. "You pathetic fools! Do you think you can vanquish the great Lucrezia Borgia? Go back into your portraits and don't bother me further."

Daniella suddenly pivoted and stepped behind Lily, throwing one arm across Lily's throat and clutching her around the waist with her other hand. Lily felt the pressure on her airway tighten as Daniella dragged her to the edge of the building once more.

Stay calm. Be brave. Lily willed herself to be strong. She didn't want to end up like the desperate girls in the portraits.

"I'm not afraid of you!" Lily shouted. "Go away!"

Daniella only chuckled and then opened her

mouth wide. "Once I take in your youth and strength these spirits will be no match for me."

Daniella was right. Lily was young and strong. And it wasn't too late for her.

With a quick motion, Lily banged her head back so that her back skull crashed into Daniella's nose. With a screech Daniella let go of Lily, tottering backward.

Lily whirled toward the spirits. "This is your chance. Take back what she's stolen from you," she shouted.

The five ghosts surrounded Daniella. They opened their mouths as something like a white mist traveled from Daniella back into their mouths. Daniella screeched and convulsed on the ground but was powerless to stop it.

In a few minutes Lily was kneeling and inhaling deeply as the stream of her life force returned to her. Looking around, she saw that the ghosts were no longer haggard, but appeared now as the beautiful young women they had been before Daniella trapped their souls with a pair of pearl earrings.

Swirls of yellow and green light shot from Daniella's body as the souls of the other young women hovering in the air were returned to them. One by one they rose up onto the roof wall, standing there, once more young and restored to their beauty. The ledge became so crowded, some hovered in the air. Before too long, there was nothing left of Daniella but a pile of ash and two pearls. And then the earrings popped and shriveled into nothing.

Lily stood staring at the five remaining ghost girls. "We tried to warn you," Julia said.

"We did," Emily agreed.

"Thank you," Lily told them.

And a thunderous banging came from the other side of the roof door.

27

Audreen and Amy burst through the door the moment Lily opened it. "Lily!" Amy cried. "Are you all right?"

Only then did Lily understand that she was finally safe and begin to cry. She buried her head in Amy's shoulder and let the tears fall. "Yes! Yes! I'm all right. She made me really old and then she was going to throw me off the roof."

"Where'd she go?" Audreen asked.

Lily pointed at the pile of ashes.

"Who — are they?" Amy asked, glancing at the girls in beautiful antique costumes.

"I know," Audreen said. "This is Ashlynne and Emily and Rosalie and Anne and Julia. And these girls must be other victims."

Once more, Lily was aware of the beating of hearts, but now the air was warm again.

"The spirits were trying to warn me," Lily now understood. "They knew what Daniella would do to me."

"You saved them," Audreen said. "When you touched Julia's portrait, you awakened her at just the same moment Daniella was growing old. What was left of her spirit was trapped in her portrait. Even though her youth and vitality had been sucked out of her and trapped in those awful earrings, your touch enabled her to get free. And she, in turn, freed the rest of the girls who had suffered the same fate."

"Well, we saved Lily, too," Julia said. "If we hadn't shown up when we did, she would have also been trapped in a portrait."

Audreen pulled the sage from her back pocket and lit it with a lighter. She began a gentle chant. "This is a chant used by the Algonquin people for the passing of the spirits into the next world," she explained as she walked around the roof waving the smokey sage. "Spirits, join hands."

At Audreen's words, the ghost girls clasped hands.

Audreen spoke the Native American language, which Lily couldn't understand, but the words didn't seem important. The meaning was clear. Audreen was easing the girls over to their next experience.

In the next ten minutes, every spirit had lifted into the sky and disappeared.

"I'm so glad you're safe," Amy said, once the three of them were alone on the roof once more.

"How did you two know to come here?" Lily asked.

"One of the spirits wrote a note to me on my wall," Audreen said. "She wrote 'Save Lily' in blood. It definitely got my attention, and I called Amy to try to find where you had gone."

"You didn't need us though," Amy said. "You handled it yourself."

Lily nodded. "I did — with a lot of help from five friends."

ABOUT THE AUTHOR

Sʋᴢᴀɴɴᴇ Wᴇʏɴ lives in a valley in New York State. She's the author of The Haunted Museum series, The Bar Code series, and the novels *Distant Waves*, *Dr. Frankenstein's Daughters*, and *Faces of the Dead* for older readers, and the Breyer Stablemates books *Diamond* and *Snowflake* for younger readers.